LUNCH BOX LIBRARY™

• READ WHILE YOU EAT •

9 Puzzle-Mysteries

BY ANDREW GUTELLE

WORKMAN PUBLISHING • NEW YORK

GOOD READING GOES WITH GOOD EATING

Lunch Box Library™ puzzles are fun for reluctant readers and speed demons alike. In *9 Puzzle-Mysteries,* children solve a different puzzle every day—including scrambles, cryptograms, math problems, and geography mazes. Each puzzle page moves the ten-part mystery along just enough so that readers will be eager to find out what happens next. Before they know it, they're hooked!

Your child can enjoy Lunch Box Library puzzle-mysteries even if he or she buys school lunch: Just tuck a puzzle in a backpack, notebook, or coat pocket. And Lunch Box Library isn't only for lunch. After breakfast, after school with a snack, in the car, or before bed—any time is a good time to solve a puzzle. Here's how it works.

Tear off the title page and "Day One" page from the first mystery, fold them in half, write a note on the back if you wish, and pack them in your child's lunch bag or box. The next morning, include "Day Two" with lunch, and so on.

There are ten puzzles in each of the nine mysteries, so each mystery will last for as many as two weeks of school lunches. Easier puzzles alternate with more difficult ones, and answers are provided on the back of each page so young sleuths won't feel frustrated if they're stumped. Fold the page so the answer doesn't show, and don't forget to include a pencil with lunch.

YOU CAN USE LUNCH BOX LIBRARY IN MANY WAYS

TO ENCOURAGE READING—A book can seem like too big a project for some young readers to tackle. Lunch Box Library is broken into digestible, one-page servings, evenly divided between reading and puzzling.

TO KEEP IN TOUCH DURING A LONG DAY APART—Many parents say they'd like to include a personal note in their child's lunch but are just too rushed in the morning.

Each episode provides space on the back for you to write your child a short note.

AS A REWARD FOR GETTING READY FOR SCHOOL ON TIME—Try hiding an episode under a pile of clean laundry as a reward for putting it away. Or ask your child to read a page aloud as you're preparing dinner or before bedtime.

TO SHARE—It's not just for school lunch. Pack an episode in a summer day-camp lunch or mail episodes to your child when you're away on business. Suggest sending puzzles to pen pals or grandparents. Children will enjoy sharing these puzzles with their friends and classmates, with their teachers, and with you.

THE CASE OF THE DISAPPEARING DOGS
A SCOTT LINYARD PUZZLE MYSTERY

> Follow Scott Linyard as he tracks down Carlotta's dogs one by one. The case will be closed when Scott catches up with ten different dog breeds.

My name is Linyard—Scott Linyard. I'm a private eye. There isn't a puzzle I can't unravel or a mystery I can't solve. I'm not bragging, that's just the way it is.

The other morning I sat at my desk enjoying my usual breakfast—donuts and cocoa. In walked Carlotta Furball, owner of Pets Etc.

"Good morning, Carlotta," I said calmly. "Care for a donut?"

"Scott, you have got to help me!" she cried. "I was at the store an hour ago. I had just come back from walking the dogs. I was in the back testing some new scratching posts when something terrible happened!

"I must have left the door open. Before I knew it ten of my prize puppies had run away! Scott, I have got to get them back!"

"I'm no dogcatcher," I said.

"Scott, you're my only hope. Please?" she purred.

I thought it over. Business was moving slower than a snail crossing a sidewalk. If I didn't make some money soon, I would be on the sidewalk too. Besides Carlotta had helped me when Pookie, my canary, had a sore throat.

"Okay," I said. "I'll do it."

THE PLOT

Scott Linyard is on a new case. He has agreed to find Carlotta Furball's ten missing dogs.

STORE SCRAMBLE

DAY ·1·

To help Carlotta, I had to act fast. By now those little bowwows could be halfway to Muttville.

The first thing you learn in detective school is to check out the crime scene. So I hurried over to Pets Etc. and had a look around. To the right of the cash register was a box of dog whistles. I picked one up and turned it over and over in my fingers. Then I put the whistle to my lips and sent a blast of air through it. Suddenly I heard barking from behind a sack of dog food.

"Carlotta," I thought, "I just found one of your dogs!"

WHICH DOG WAS IT? Unscramble the letters to find six items that you might buy for a pet dog. Then read the letters in the circles from top to bottom.

1. BISTUCI ◯ __ __ __ __ __

2. HEALS __ ◯ __ __ __

3. LOCLAR __ __ __ ◯ __

4. GDO SEOUH __ __ ◯ __ __ __ __ __

5. OLBW __ __ __ ◯

6. NEESCIL __ __ __ __ ◯ __ __

__ __ __ __ __ __

ANSWERS ON THE BACK

LUNCH BOX DAY .1. LIBRARY

ANSWER:
1. Biscuit
2. Leash
3. Collar
4. Dog house
5. Bowl
6. License

The circled letters spell the word BEAGLE

SIGN SIGNAL

SO FAR

Yesterday Scott found a beagle at Pets Etc., but there are still nine dogs missing.

To find a dog you need to think like a dog. So next I went where a smart dog would go—to Alpine's Butcher Shop. I heard growling inside but it wasn't a dog. It was Alvin Alpine the owner.

"I caught 'im, I did," barked Alvin. "No dog tries to take my bones and gets away with it!"

"Thanks, Alvin," I said, as he handed me dog number two.

WHICH DOG DID ALVIN CATCH? Take a look at the butcher's sign. Follow each line from a letter until you reach a box. Write that letter in the box. The letters will spell your answer.

ANSWERS ON THE BACK

LUNCH BOX **DAY · 2 ·** LIBRARY

LUNCH NOTES:

_____

_____

_____

_____

_____

_____

_____

ANSWER: Spaniel

DOGS FOUND SO FAR:
1. Beagle
2. Spaniel

FILL-IN STATION

DAY
· 3 ·

SO FAR

Scott snared a spaniel at Alpine's Butcher Shop. Where shoud he go next?

I drove all over town without much luck. I was running on empty and so was my car, so I pulled into Gussie's Gas. While Gussie worked the pump, I pumped her for information.

"Strangest thing," she said. "Something chewed through a brand-new tire in the back of the garage."

A tire chewer? I ran inside and collared dog number three!

WHICH DOG WAS IN THE GAS STATION? Use the clues to fill in the words. Then match the letters to the numbers below.

1. Opposite of over: $\overline{}_{8} \ \overline{}_{17} \ \overline{}_{10} \ \overline{}_{20} \ \overline{}_{14}$

2. Frankfurters: $\overline{}_{19} \ \overline{}_{7} \ \overline{}_{4} \ \ \overline{}_{25} \ \overline{}_{3} \ \overline{}_{12} \ \overline{}_{1}$

3. Home for cows and crops: $\overline{}_{6} \ \overline{}_{11} \ \overline{}_{24} \ \overline{}_{15}$

4. Stars and moons are in outer _____: $\overline{}_{18} \ \overline{}_{21} \ \overline{}_{16} \ \overline{}_{2} \ \overline{}_{13}$

5. Now and _____: $\overline{}_{5} \ \overline{}_{22} \ \overline{}_{23} \ \overline{}_{9}$

$\overline{}_{1} \ \overline{}_{2} \ \overline{}_{3} \ \overline{}_{4} \ \overline{}_{5} \quad \overline{}_{6} \ \overline{}_{7} \ \overline{}_{8} \ \overline{}_{9} \ \overline{}_{10} \quad \overline{}_{11}$

$\overline{}_{12} \ \overline{}_{13} \ \overline{}_{14} \ \overline{}_{15} \ \overline{}_{16} \ \overline{}_{17}$

$\overline{}_{18} \ \overline{}_{19} \ \overline{}_{20} \ \overline{}_{21} \ \overline{}_{22} \ \overline{}_{23} \ \overline{}_{24} \ \overline{}_{25}$

ANSWERS ON THE BACK

LUNCH NOTES:

ANSWER:
1. Under
2. Hot dogs
3. Farm
4. Space
5. Then

Scott found a German Shepherd

DOGS FOUND SO FAR:
1. Beagle
2. Spaniel
3. German Shepherd

POODLE PAIRS

SO FAR

A German shepherd was chewing tires at Gussie's Gas. That's three dogs caught and seven to go!

On a hunch, I hustled over to Fern's Fur-cuts—the best pet barbershop in town. Actually it was the only one in town. I found Fern in a frenzy.

"Scott, it just doesn't make sense," she exclaimed. "I am supposed to give eight poodles haircuts, but there are nine in the shop."

"Say no more," I told her. "I'll take it from here."

FIND THE ONE POODLE THAT DOES NOT HAVE A MATCH.

ANSWERS ON THE BACK

LUNCH BOX **DAY · 4 ·** LIBRARY

LUNCH NOTES:

_____

_____

_____

_____

_____

_____

_____

ANSWER: The poodle on the upper right.

DOGS FOUND SO FAR:
1. Beagle
2. Spaniel
3. German Shepherd
4. Poodle

SO FAR

Scott picked up a poodle at Fern's Fur-cuts. Four of Carlotta's ten dogs have now been found.

DISAPPEARING DOGS

LETTER MAN

DAY 5

There was one man who knew every pooch in town: Phil the postman. I found him stuffing a mailbox on De Soto Drive.

I filled in Phil. "I thought something was up," he said. "I saw a dog I didn't recognize. He was sleeping under an elm tree on Maple Street."

Maple Street

WHICH DOG WAS IT? Use these clues to find the answer. Write each letter in the correct space to spell its name.

1. The first letter is in DUCK but not in QUACK
2. The second letter is the only vowel not found in this sentence
3. The third letter is the fifth consonant in INSTRUCTIONS
4. Letter four is in MARCH but in no other month
5. Letter five is the only consonant in the UNITED STATES OF AMERICA to begin and end a word
6. The sixth letter is the eighteenth one in this sentence
7. The seventh letter is in OCTOPUS and SQUID but not CATFISH
8. The eighth letter is always in SUNDAY but never in THURSDAY
9. The ninth letter is in the middle of GRIDDLE

___ ___ ___ ___ ___ ___ ___ ___ ___
 1   2   3   4   5   6   7   8   9

ANSWERS ON THE BACK

LUNCH BOX **DAY · 5 ·** LIBRARY

LUNCH NOTES:

_____

_____

_____

_____

_____

_____

_____

ANSWER: Dachshund

DOGS FOUND SO FAR:
1. Beagle
2. Spaniel
3. German Shepherd
4. Poodle
5. Dachshund

BY THE NUMBERS

DAY · 6

The trail was getting colder than a bucket of ice cubes. I decided to visit Fuzzy Sanders over at the zoo. I found Fuzzy giving a penguin a bird bath.

"You're in luck, Scott," he said. "I found a four-legged trespasser this morning. I caught him pestering my puffins. He's cooling his paws in my office."

SCRATCH PAD

WHICH ANSWER IS THE LARGEST? Solve each of these three multiplication problems. Write the answers below. The largest number leads to the dog Scott found at the zoo.

1. Multiply the number of legs on a spider times the number of keys on a piano

2. Multiply the number of innings in a baseball game times the number of cards in a deck

3. Multiply the number of states in the U.S.A. times a baker's dozen

1. _____ ☞ COLLIE

2. _____ ☞ GREYHOUND

3. _____ ☞ SHEEPDOG

ANSWERS ON THE BACK

LUNCH NOTES:

ANSWER:
1. 8 X 88 = 704
2. 9 X 52 = 468
3. 13 X 50 = 650

Scott found a collie

DOGS FOUND SO FAR:
1. Beagle
2. Spaniel
3. German Shepherd
4. Poodle
5. Dachshund
6. Collie

CYCLE CODE

SO FAR

Yesterday Scott collared a collie at the town zoo. He still needs to find four more dogs.

I was really on a roll. I decided to visit Ike's Cycle Shop next. By now the news of my case had spread all over town. Ike was waiting with my latest clue.

"I was out riding a ten-speed this morning. Suddenly some strange dog started barking at my back wheel. It followed me back to the shop. It's in the garage right now!"

USE THE WHEEL TO FIND THE DOG. Begin at START. Write that letter in the space below. Now count three spaces clockwise. Write the letter you find in the next space. Keep counting three spaces at a time until you have used all the letters.

START

__ __ __ __ __ __

__ __ __ __ __ __ __

ANSWERS ON THE BACK

LUNCH BOX **DAY · 7 ·** LIBRARY

LUNCH NOTES:

_____

_____

_____

_____

_____

_____

_____

ANSWER: a Golden Retriever

DOGS FOUND SO FAR:
1. Beagle
2. Spaniel
3. German Shepherd
4. Poodle
5. Dachshund
6. Collie
7. Golden Retriever

DOG BYTES

DAY
·8·

SO FAR

Scott picked up a golden retriever to bring his total to seven dogs. Now he must find dog number eight.

I decided to check back with my office. It turned out to be a great idea. There was an important message waiting for me in my electronic mailbox. It was from the town hacker—C.D. Ramona: "Good news, Scott. Another dog has been found."

The rest of her message was about as clear as a desert sandstorm. I had to crack her code to collar that canine.

WHAT DID THE MESSAGE SAY? To figure out C. D. Ramona's message you must first do three things:

1. Cross out the words that rhyme with plane

2. Cross out the numbers

3. Cross out the words that begin with B or S

Now read the leftover letters.

4 starters the main 500 barking dog bulldog 808 is a small Boxer sitting behind greyhound. bus pick slippery her Saint 11 Bernard 13 british bananas 1997 train up boxcars 500 rain at setter my bloodhound house.

ANSWERS ON THE BACK

LUNCH BOX **DAY · 8 ·** LIBRARY

ANSWER: The dog is a greyhound. Pick her up at my house.

DOGS FOUND SO FAR:
1. Beagle
2. Spaniel
3. German Shepherd
4. Poodle
5. Dachshund
6. Collie
7. Golden Retriever
8. Greyhound

A CAPITAL IDEA

DAY · 9 ·

SO FAR

With the help of C.D. Ramona, Scott found a greyhound. That's eight dogs down and two to go!

The day was nearly over and I was running out of leads. I decided a little research might help so I hustled over to the town library. I was looking for the pet books section when I heard the patter of paws behind me. I was being followed!

I ducked down an aisle and buried my nose in a book. When I peered through the shelves of books I spotted dog number nine!

WHICH DOG WAS IT? Here is a list of capitals. Write the correct state next to each capital. Then read the first letters of the states in order. They spell the name of the dog.

1. DOVER

2. JUNEAU

3. BATON ROUGE

4. BOSTON

5. LITTLE ROCK

6. AUSTIN

7. SPRINGFIELD

8. MONTGOMERY

9. LINCOLN

— — — — — — — — —

ANSWERS ON THE BACK

LUNCH NOTES:

ANSWER:
1. Delaware
2. Alaska
3. Louisiana
4. Massachusetts
5. Arkansas
6. Texas
7. Illinois
8. Alabama
9. Nebraska.

Scott found a dalmatian

DOGS FOUND SO FAR:
1. Beagle
2. Spaniel
3. German Shepherd
4. Poodle
5. Dachshund
6. Collie
7. Golden Retriever
8. Greyhound
9. Dalmatian

CASE CLOSED!

I was dog tired but I couldn't give up. I was one mutt away from closing out this caper. That's when my cell phone started squawking. It was my message service calling. Carlotta Furball had telephoned. She wanted me to hustle over to Pets Etc.

When I arrived at the store Carlotta was waiting for me. She held a little pooch in her paws.

"The last dog?" I asked.

Carlotta nodded. "I guess she got hungry or homesick . . . or both."

"Nothing beats a happy ending," I said coolly.

The case was closed. I was about to ask Carlotta for my money when she handed me a note. Doggone it!

To read the message, replace each letter with the one that comes before it in the alphabet. (Hint: For instance Tdpuu = Scott.)

Tdpuu,

Uibolt gps zpvs ifmq. Tjodf J epo'u ibwf boz npofz up qbz zpv, J xbou up hjwf zpv eph ovncfs ufo. J ipqf zpv mjlf uijt mjuumf dijivbivb.

Mpwf,

Dbsmpuub

ANSWERS ON THE BACK

LUNCH NOTES:

ANSWER:

Scott,

Thanks for your help. Since I don't have any money to pay you,

I want to give you dog number ten.

I hope you like this little Chihuahua.

Love,

Carlotta

DOGS FOUND SO FAR:

1. Beagle
2. Spaniel
3. German Shepherd
4. Poodle
5. Dachshund
6. Collie
7. Golden Retriever
8. Greyhound
9. Dalmatian
10. Chihuahua

DEADLINE FOR HEADLINES
AN INKY O'BRIEN PUZZLE MYSTERY

> Join Inky O'Brien as she races around town gathering news for the *Downtown Gazette*. Solve puzzles that write the headlines for her nine stories.

My name is Ingrid O'Brien, but everyone calls me Inky. I'm a reporter for the *Downtown Gazette*. When a story breaks in town, I get the news fast and first.

Of course I wasn't always a big-shot reporter. In fact my first job was pretty dull. I did odd jobs at the *Gazette*. I wrote the answers for the crossword puzzles and typed the weekly school lunch menu. (Who eats that stuff?) I didn't mind, though. I was waiting for my chance.

My big break came during the annual *Gazette* picnic. On that day the staff parties on Elk Island. It's a day of fun for everyone—except for the person left behind to mind the office. As usual, I was that person.

I was relaxing in my boss's chair when the phone rang suddenly. My boss, Scoop Johnson, was calling. "It's a disaster!" he shouted. "It's those darn elk. One of them chewed through the rope holding our boat at the dock. The boat is drifting in the middle of the bay!"

Getting stuck on beautiful Elk Island didn't seem so bad to me. Then I realized the problem. If the reporters were stuck, who would get stories for tomorrow's paper?

"Don't worry, Boss," I said confidently. "I'll take care of everything." With that I hung up the phone, grabbed my coat, and raced out the door.

PEACH PROBLEM

DAY
· 1 ·

THE PLOT

Inky O'Brien must gather nine stories to fill the *Downtown Gazette*. Solve puzzles to help her write headlines.

I left the office with a list of possible stories around town. At the top was a note to visit Fanny Popper's farm. Fanny grows the best peaches in the county.

I found Fanny at her farm surrounded by her fabulous fruit. There were plums, pears, melons, but no peaches.

"I goofed," she said sadly. "It was that cold weekend weather. I started picking fruit as fast as I could. By the time I reached the peaches it was too late!"

I scribbled words on my notepad. When Fanny Popper finished speaking, I had my first story!

TO WRITE THE FIRST HEADLINE CHECK INKY'S NOTES. Take the first letter from each word. Write those first letters in order in the spaces below.

Pears okay. Plums

seem terrific. Only

peaches crummy, right?

Oh! Poor Fanny left out

peaches Sunday.

__ __ __ ' __

__ __ __

__ __ __

__ __ __ __

ANSWERS ON THE BACK

LUNCH BOX **DAY · 1 ·** LIBRARY

ANSWER: Pop's Top Crop Flops

SNORING SHEEP

DAY 2

SO FAR

Yesterday Inky got her first story. She must gather eight more to fill the *Downtown Gazette*.

As I drove past Woolly Saunders's sheep ranch, I saw something that made me stop my car. Woolly's flock was sound asleep. In the middle of the herd was a Jeep.

"Strangest thing," said Woolly. "I bought that old Jeep the other day. It can't move, but my sheep like it. The hum of the motor keeps 'em snoozing all day."

My editor loved weird stories like this one! I asked Woolly for all the details.

FILL IN THE CORRECT ONE-WORD ANSWER FOR EACH CLUE. Then write the numbered letters below to complete Inky's second headline.

1. Clothes you sleep in: __ __ __ __ __ __
           1   2

2. Lights on a birthday cake: __ __ __ __ __ __ __
          3 4

3. Cucumbers that turn sour: __ __ __ __ __ __
          5   6

4. Sweet bee food: __ __ __ __ __
        7   8

___ ___ ___ ___ ___   ___ ___ ___ ___   ___ ___ ___ ___ ___
3 7 8 4 5   1 8 8 5   7 8 6 5 2

___ ___ ___ ___ ___   ___ ___ ___ ___ ___
2 7 8 8 5   2 6 8 8 5

LUNCH BOX **DAY · 2 ·** LIBRARY

LUNCH NOTES:

ANSWER:
1. Pajamas
2. Candles
3. Pickles
4. Honey

Cheap Jeep Helps Sheep Sleep

EASY AS PIE?

DAY 3

SO FAR

Inky's found two stories in the weirdest places.

My next stop was the county airport. The Feather-Light Pie Company was holding its annual stunt flying contest. The winner would get a giant banana cream pie.

Up above, Ace Hardy and Wings Hutton flew spectacular loop-de-loops in their airplanes. However, the wildest action was on the ground. The two judges were arguing about who should win. One wanted to give the award to Ace. The other insisted it go to Wings.

I watched the action above me and the action on the ground. Pretty soon I knew how this story would turn out.

TO WRITE YOUR HEADLINE, FIND ALL THE SUMS UNDER 200. Then write the words that go with them from the smallest number to the largest.

1. FLY (2 X 67=?) _____
2. FOR (13 X 12=?) _____
3. GUYS (51 X 3=?) _____
4. HIGH (9 X 27=?) _____
5. PIE (4 X 44=?) _____
6. PRIZE (39 X 5=?) _____
7. SKY (8 X 29=?) _____
8. SURPRISE (6 X 40=?) _____
9. TIE (11 X 14=?) _____
10. WISE (33 X 7=?) _____

_____ _____ _____

_____ _____ _____

ANSWERS ON THE BACK

LUNCH BOX **DAY 3** LIBRARY

LUNCH NOTES:

ANSWER:
1. FLY = 134
2. FOR = 156
3. GUYS = 153
4. HIGH = 243
5. PIE = 176
6. PRIZE = 195
7. SKY = 232
8. SURPRISE = 240
9. TIE = 154
10. WISE = 231

Fly Guys Tie For Pie Prize

DOGGONE IT!

DAY 4

SO FAR

Inky has picked up three of the nine stories she needs. Today she is after the fourth.

The county fairgrounds are at the edge of town. I stopped there to get the scoop on this week's championship dog show.

It was raining cats and dogs when I arrived. I folded my umbrella and went inside. I found Dwayne Scott with his dog, a Great Dane named Spot. He was wrapping Spot's leg in a bandage. "It's this darn weather," complained Dwayne. Spot tried to avoid a poodle and slipped in a puddle!"

TO WRITE THE HEADLINE USE THE CLUES TO FIND EACH LETTER. Then write the letters in the spaces below.

1. Letter 1 appears in the name of every month in fall and winter
2. Letter 2 is the only vowel not found in this sentence
3. Letter 3 is also the number 1 in Roman numerals
4. Letter 4 is in the middle of TORNADO
5. Letter 5 is the sixteenth one of the alphabet
6. Letter 6 is in ASIA and AUSTRALIA, but not ANTARCTICA
7. Letter 7 comes in the alphabet just before the second vowel
8. Letter 8 has the longest name of any letter in the alphabet
9. Letter 9 appears one time only in each day of the week
10. Letter 10 is in EAST and WEST but not NORTH or SOUTH

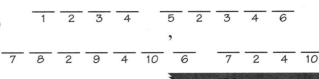

$\overline{}_{1} \ \overline{}_{2} \ \overline{}_{3} \ \overline{}_{4} \quad \overline{}_{5} \ \overline{}_{2} \ \overline{}_{3} \ \overline{}_{4} \ \overline{}_{6}$

,

$\overline{}_{7} \ \overline{}_{8} \ \overline{}_{2} \ \overline{}_{9} \ \overline{}_{4} \ \overline{}_{10} \ \overline{}_{6} \quad \overline{}_{7} \ \overline{}_{2} \ \overline{}_{4} \ \overline{}_{10}$

ANSWERS ON THE BACK

LUNCH BOX DAY · 4 · LIBRARY

LUNCH NOTES:

ANSWER: Rain Pains Dwayne's Dane

CIRCUS RUCKUS

SO FAR

Inky has four of the stories she needs to fill the newspaper. Here comes number five!

The circus was in town. The *Gazette* always runs a behind-the-scenes story so I went there next.

I didn't find clowns, jugglers, or acrobats inside the circus tent. Instead I discovered Lydia the Eel Woman arguing with Neal Dinks, the seal trainer.

It seemed that Binky the seal had eaten a bucket of fish that belonged to an eel named Slinky. While Binky barked and Slinky slithered, I wrote my story.

TO WRITE THE HEADLINE, START IN A BOX WITH A LETTER. Follow the arrow from the letter to an empty box. Write the same letter in that box. Keep going until you have filled in all the boxes.

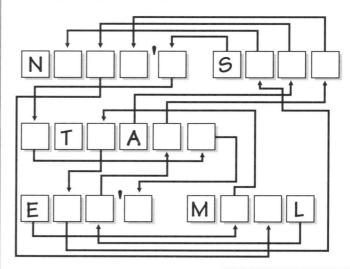

LUNCH BOX DAY ·5· LIBRARY

LUNCH NOTES:

_____

_____

_____

_____

_____

_____

_____

ANSWER: Neal's Seal Steals Eel's Meal

SILLY RABBIT

DAY 6

My next stop was the courthouse. Millionaire Matilda "Sunny" Weathers died last month. Today attorney Bill Bumper was reading her will. It was time to find out who would get her money.

Sunny's relatives were gloomy. Apparently she had left her fortune to her pet rabbit Thumper. As the bunny hopped around the courthouse doing tricks I could see why Sunny loved Thumper. The silly rabbit made Bill Bumper laugh. Soon I was smiling, too.

USE THE TIC-TAC-TOE CODE TO WRITE THE NEXT HEADLINE. Find each matching shape. If there is no dot, use the first letter from that shape. If there is a dot, use the second letter in the shape. Some are done to get you started.

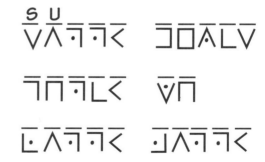

ANSWERS ON THE BACK

LUNCH BOX **DAY 6** LIBRARY

LUNCH NOTES:

_____

_____

_____

_____

_____

_____

_____

ANSWER: Sunny Gives Money To Funny Bunny

SO FAR

Six stories are set for the *Downtown Gazette*. Inky needs three more.

HEE-HAW!

My next stop was the board of education. Parents and teachers were there, so were several students, including Yul Berry. Every day Yul rode his mule, Rosebud, from his farm to school. He "parked" her in the school yard where Rosebud caused lots of trouble. Last week she ate the school compost heap. The school board took a vote. Their decision? No mules allowed!

WHAT IS THE NEXT HEADLINE? Use the clues to fill in the words. Then match the letters to the numbers below.

1. It's used to write on blackboards: ___ ___ ___ ___ ___
   16 17 12 3 13

2. Opposite of winner: ___ ___ ___ ___ ___
   20 19 14 11 21

3. Mickey or Minnie: ___ ___ ___ ___ ___
   5 18 2 15 8

4. Kid who picks on other kids: ___ ___ ___ ___ ___
   9 6 7 23 1

5. Word that means "certain": ___ ___ ___ ___
   4 22 10 24

___ ___ ___ ___ ___ ___ ___ ___
1   2   3   4   5   6   7   8

___ ___ ___ ___ ___ ___ ___ ___ ___ ___ ___
16 12 2 15 11 4   15 16 17 18 19 20

___ ___ ___ ___
21 22 23 24

ANSWERS ON THE BACK

LUNCH BOX · DAY 7 · LIBRARY

ANSWER:
1. Chalk
2. Loser
3. Mouse
4. Bully
5. Sure

Yul's Mule Causes School Rule

LETTER SWAP

SO FAR

Inky needs two more stories. Will she get a job as a reporter when she finishes?

checked my watch. By now the reporters would be rescued from Elk Island. Soon they would be back at the *Gazette* offices. I needed two more stories and I needed them fast.

My next stop was the annual Miss String Bean Contest. I watched Norma Jean Jenkins in action. She sang a song. She tap-danced. She whipped up a string bean soufflé. I saw the judges place a crown of string beans on her head. Then I made my notes for another story.

TO WRITE THE NEXT HEADLINE USE THE LETTER PAIRS AT OPPOSITE ENDS OF EACH STRING BEAN. Switch each letter with its partner to complete the headline.

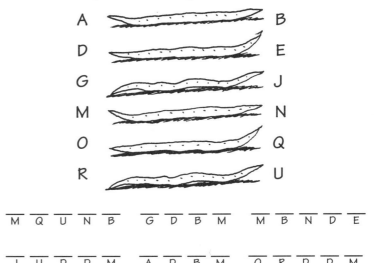

$\overline{M}\ \overline{Q}\ \overline{U}\ \overline{N}\ \overline{B}$ $\overline{G}\ \overline{D}\ \overline{B}\ \overline{M}$ $\overline{M}\ \overline{B}\ \overline{N}\ \overline{D}\ \overline{E}$

$\overline{J}\ \overline{U}\ \overline{D}\ \overline{D}\ \overline{M}$ $\overline{A}\ \overline{D}\ \overline{B}\ \overline{M}$ $\overline{O}\ \overline{R}\ \overline{D}\ \overline{D}\ \overline{M}$

ANSWERS ON THE BACK

LUNCH BOX **DAY · 8 ·** LIBRARY

ANSWER: Norma Jean Named Green Bean Queen

JUMBLE CRUMBLE

SO FAR

Inky needs to get one final story and make it back to the office of the *Downtown Gazette.*

It was getting late. I realized I hadn't had anything to eat all day. I decided to stop at Royal Roy's Ice Cream Stand for a quick banana split. Royal Roy's was a town landmark. His sign—a tall wooden crown covered with fake chocolate sauce—could be seen for miles.

Or could it? As I pulled into the parking lot I saw Royal Roy surrounded by pieces of wood. His giant chocolate crown had crumbled! "Termites," he said sadly.

I got my banana split and my final story to go!

FIND THE LETTERS THAT ARE WRITTEN IN THE SAME KIND OF LETTERING. You will have four groups of letters. Unscramble each group to make a word. Then turn them into a headline. *(Hint: three of the words rhyme.)*

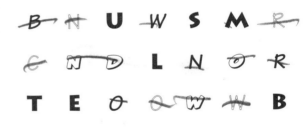

brown crown
tumbles down

ANSWERS ON THE BACK

LUNCH BOX DAY 9 LIBRARY

_____

_____

_____

_____

_____

_____

_____

ANSWER: Brown Crown Tumbles Down

START THE PRESSES

SO FAR

Inky has all nine stories. Will her boss finally give her a job as a reporter?

I was already working at my desk when the reporters returned. Scoop Johnson led them into the newsroom.

"You're just in time," I said.

Scoop glared at me. "You were supposed to be here at the office. I tried to call you all afternoon . . ."

Just then he saw the final story on my computer screen. Scoop hit the send button on my computer and walked into his office to read my stories in private.

I sat and waited. Was he still mad at me? Would I lose my job? Did he like my stories?

Finally Scoop came out of his office. He dropped a stack of papers on my desk. There were nine stories ready to go and the tenth one just for me.

TO WRITE THE FINAL HEADLINE COPY THE FIVE WORDS FROM THE STORY. The words are indicated below.

There was quite a fuss today when the *Downtown Gazette* news boat was set adrift in the inky black waters off Elk Island. The problem was linked to a hungry elk who chewed through the rope holding the boat. A coast guard crew came to the rescue. Fortunately disaster was averted. Star reporter Ingrid O'Brien gathered enough news to fill this special edition.

WORD #18	WORD #27	WORD #45	WORD #58

WORD #43

ANSWERS ON THE BACK

LUNCH BOX DAY 10 LIBRARY

LUNCH NOTES:

_____

_____

_____

_____

_____

_____

_____

ANSWER: Inky Linked To News Crew

THE SEARCH FOR WRONGWAY FARADAY

A JACK DAKOTA PUZZLE MYSTERY

Join Jack Dakota as he travels the world on the trail of Wrongway Faraday. Solve puzzles to help Jack journey from one place to the next.

My name is Jack Dakota and I love adventure. If you want to go fishing in Wales or bowling in Bolivia, I can take you there.

I never know when I'm about to begin an adventure. Take the other day, for example. I was down at city hall picking up my new passport. Who should I see, but my old classmate Leslie Faraday. Normally Leslie is a cool customer but today she was plenty upset.

"Hey, Les, what's cooking?" I asked.

"Jack," she cried. "Just the person I need. Dad's done it again!"

Leslie's father, Irwin Faraday, was a famous traveler. Unfortunately, he couldn't cross the street without getting lost. Irwin once went to the store to buy a pint of ice cream and ended up in Iceland. After that, people started calling him "Wrongway" Faraday.

Leslie handed me a postcard her father had sent her: "Having a wonderful time in Egypt. Hope to see the pyramids today."

I turned it over. The picture on the postcard showed a very handsome kangaroo, beneath it were the words "Welcome to Australia."

"He's lost again," sighed Leslie.

I was tired of hanging around the office. I grabbed my passport and gave Leslie a kiss on the cheek. "Don't worry," I said. "I'll find him!"

AUSTRALIA TRAIL

DAY · 1 ·

THE PLOT

Jack Dakota must find Irwin "Wrong-way" Faraday who is lost somewhere in the world.

I took a night flight to Australia. The next morning I arrived in the city of Sydney. My old friend Matilda Walters was waiting at the hotel. Matty and I had led a camel safari across Australia years ago.

I showed her Wrongway's postcard. "They sell these over at the zoo," she said. "Let's start there."

In front of the zoo we found a guy named Kangaroo Charlie selling postcards. "I saw your mate," he laughed. "Funny old bloke—he said he was going to Canada but that ain't what his ticket said!"

WHERE WAS WRONGWAY GOING NEXT? Use these clues to find the answer. Write each letter in the correct space to spell the name of the country.

1. The first letter appears exactly one time each in OCTOBER, DECEMBER and FEBRUARY

2. The second letter appears more than any other in GREAT BARRIER REEF

3. The third letter begins and ends the name of the country where Jack is right now

4. Turn an N on its side to see the fourth letter

5. The fifth letter is the only vowel not in THE LAND DOWN UNDER

6. The last letter is in KOALA but *not* in KANGAROO

THE NEXT COUNTRY IS

___ ___ ___ ___ ___ ___
1   2   3   4   5   6

ANSWERS ON THE BACK

LUNCH BOX **DAY · 1 ·** LIBRARY

LUNCH NOTES:

_____

_____

_____

_____

_____

_____

_____

ANSWER: Brazil

WRONGWAY'S TRIP SO FAR:
1. Australia
2. Brazil

MIXED MESSAGE

DAY 2

SO FAR

Jack Dakota knows Wrongway Faraday went from Australia to Brazil. Where will he go next?

I was exhausted when I landed in Brazil. Fortunately it was carnival time in the city of Rio de Janeiro. If there is one thing better than a great adventure it's a great party! I joined the crowd, and we paraded through the streets of Rio. I danced the samba all night long.

The next day I planned to go sun-bathing on Copacabana Beach. Before I left, I checked my e-mail back home. I was glad I did. Leslie Faraday had some news about her missing father. All I had to do was clean up a little computer babble to read it!

CHa
CHa
CHa

WHAT DID THE MESSAGE SAY? To read the message replace the symbols with the correct vowels. (* = A, & = E, % = I and # = O.)

D*D TR%&D T# C*LL

C#LL&CT BUT W& W&R&

D%SC#NN&CT&D. % TH%NK

TH& #P&R*T#R W*S

SP&*K%NG %N CH%N&S&.

ANSWERS ON THE BACK

LUNCH BOX DAY 2 LIBRARY

LUNCH NOTES:

_____

_____

_____

_____

_____

_____

_____

ANSWER: Dad tried to call collect but we
were disconnected. I think the operator was
speaking in Chinese.

WRONGWAY'S TRIP SO FAR:
1. Australia
2. Brazil
3. China

LETTER MAZE

DAY
· 3 ·

SO FAR

Jack followed
Wrongway Faraday
to Australia, Brazil...
and now, China.
Where will he go next?

I arrived in Beijing, China, with a huge problem. How would I find Wrongway Faraday in a country with more than one billion people? I needed help.

Fortunately I had a friend at the United States embassy. She had a friend at the passport office whose uncle worked at the airport.

While they put out the word, I decided to explore the city. I had just reached Tiananmen Square when a young boy ran up to me with an important message. It was about Wrongway Faraday!

START WITH THE H IN THE TOP CORNER. Step from one letter to the next making words as you go. You may go up, down, or across from one letter to another one next to it. You can even change direction in the middle of a word. Use each letter one time to spell the message.

```
H  E  T  D  E
E  N  O  O  N
A  A  O  T  M
L  L  K  Y  A
L  P  A  A  R
T  H  E  W  K
```

ANSWERS ON THE BACK

LUNCH NOTES:

```
H E T D E
E N O O N
A A O T M
L L K Y A
L P A A R
T H E W K
```

ANSWER: He took a plane all the way to Denmark

WRONGWAY'S TRIP SO FAR:
1. Australia
2. Brazil
3. China
4. Denmark

SO FAR

WRONGWAY FARADAY

PHOTO SHOW

DAY
·4·

I was glad Faraday had departed for Denmark. Copenhagen is one of my favorite cities in the world. I decided to visit the Tivoli Gardens. I was relaxing at a sidewalk cafe when I heard a click! A photographer who took pictures of tourists had snapped mine.

I figured this shutterbug saw everyone who came through town. I showed him my snapshot of Wrongway. "Not a very good picture," he sniffed. "I took a better one of him the other day. He was getting on a bus to the airport."

WHERE WAS WRONGWAY GOING? Unscramble all these words rhyming with "owe."

1. CEOH ☐ __ __ __

2. THETOG ☐ __ __ __ __ __

3. ELLOYW ☐ __ __ __ __ __

4. LIPLOW ☐ __ __ __ __ __

5. ROOTDAN ☐ __ __ __ __ __ __

Read the first letters of the unscrambled words from 1 to 5 to discover Wrongway's destination.

THE NEXT COUNTRY IS

___ ___ ___ ___ ___
1   2   3   4   5

ANSWERS ON THE BACK

LUNCH NOTES:

ANSWER:
1. Echo
2. Ghetto
3. Yellow
4. Pillow
5. Tornado

EGYPT

WRONGWAY'S TRIP SO FAR:
1. Australia
2. Brazil
3. China
4. Denmark
5. Egypt

PYRAMID PLUS

DAY
· 5 ·

SO FAR

Jack Dakota is on his way to Egypt, the fifth country in Wrongway's journey.

I flew to Cairo, Egypt. After I landed, I made tracks to the Great Pyramid of Cheops. It was awesome. As I stood there with my mouth hanging open, someone hollered, "Jack Dakota!"

I turned, hoping to see Wrongway Faraday. Instead it was my old buddy Ali Babble. He and I had met years ago while exploring tombs along the Nile.

I told Ali why I was there. "If only I had known," he sighed. "I met Mr. Faraday yesterday. We walked the steps of the pyramid together. It was his last stop before leaving the country!"

WORK FROM BOTTOM TO TOP TO FILL IN ALL THE NUMBERS ON THE PYRAMID. Add each pair of numbers that are side by side. Write the answer in the space above the pair. Keep adding pairs until you reach the top number. The top number tells you where Jack must go next.

FIND THE TOP NUMBER BELOW:

505 = Frankfurt, Germany
506 = Paris, France
605 = Helsinki, Finland

80

27   53   76   92

ANSWERS ON THE BACK

LUNCH NOTES:

ANSWER:

```
            506
        209   297
     80   129   168
  27   53   76   92
```

506 = Paris, France

WRONGWAY'S TRIP SO FAR:

1. Australia
2. Brazil
3. China
4. Denmark
5. Egypt
6. France

JACKS ARE WILD

DAY
• 6 •

SO FAR

Jack's in France,
his favorite stop.
Where to next?

Whenever I visit Paris, France, I always begin at Chez Jacques. My favorite chef serves fabulous food. Jacques also dishes out great bits of gossip. If anyone knew where Wrongway Faraday was, it would be him.

"That scoundrel," he growled when I asked about Faraday. "I prepared a feast for him and he asked for a doggy bag! He said he had a train to catch right away!"

WHERE DID WRONGWAY GO? Use the clues to fill in all the JACK words. Then fill in the letters to find out where Wrongway went.

A toy that pops its top:
J A C K - __ __ - __ __ __ - __ __ __
        1   2   3

A halloween pumpkin:
J A C K - __ ' - __ __ __ __ __ __
       4   5   6

An exercise:
__ __ __ __ __ __ J A C K S
     7   8

A large hare:
J A C K __ __ __ __ __ __
        9   10

A make-believe winter character:
J A C K __ __ __ __ __
         11   12 13

__ __ __ __ __ __ __ __ __ __ __ __ __
13 2 5 6 5 3 13 12 13 4 7 1 12

__ __ __ __ __ __ __ __ __ __ __ __
8 11 5 9 13 10 11 1 13 9 1 6

ANSWERS ON THE BACK

LUNCH NOTES:

ANSWER:
1. Jack-in-the-box
2. Jack-o'-lantern
3. Jumping jacks
4. Jackrabbit
5. Jack Frost

The next stop is Great Britain

WRONGWAY'S TRIP SO FAR:
1. Australia
2, Brazil
3. China
4. Denmark
5. Egypt
6. France
7. Great Britain

CLOCK CODE

DAY · 7 ·

SO FAR

Jack Dakota has trailed Wrongway to Great Britain. That makes seven places. Where is number eight?

I took the train to London, England. Who should be waiting for me but my favorite cabbie—Charlie Doolittle.

I told Charlie all about Wrongway Faraday. Suddenly he reached into the glove compartment. Charlie handed me a copy of yesterday's newspaper. "Have a look at page seven," he chuckled.

There was a big picture of Wrongway. He had spent two days lost in the underground, the London subway system. Finally the police rescued him and sent him on his way.

WHERE TO NEXT? The letters on the clock are a code. Write each pair of letters the hands point to in the spaces below. Always write the large hand letter first. The first one is done to get you started.

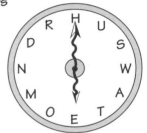

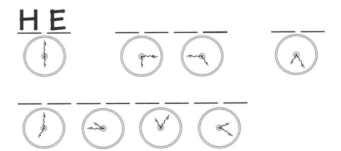

H E

ANSWERS ON THE BACK

LUNCH NOTES:

ANSWER: He went to Honduras

WRONGWAY'S TRIP SO FAR:

1. Australia
2. Brazil
3. China
4. Denmark
5. Egypt
6. France
7. Great Britain
8. Honduras

POSTCARD PUZZLE

DAY 8

My next stop was Tegucigalpa, the capital of Honduras. I decided to visit every hotel in town. If Wrongway was here he would have checked in somewhere.

I was at my fifth hotel when I got lucky. Not only had Wrongway been there, he had left behind a postcard. It was addressed to yours truly—Jack Dakota!

TO DECODE THE MESSAGE YOU MUST DO THREE THINGS:

1. Cross out the animals
2. Cross out the words that begin with S
3. Cross out the words that end in L

DEAR SILLY JACK,

STOP! I MOSQUITO PEEL UNDERSTAND FROM MY MONKEY SINCE FOOTBALL SATURDAY DAUGHTER THAT YOU ARE SLOWLY TRYING TO FIND SIX ELEPHANTS THRILL ME. I DON'T JAIL KNOW SLIPPERY ZEBRA WHY PEOPLE NAMED ME SLIMY MOOSE WRONGWAY. THERE IS A DULL PLAN TO MY EVIL SUPERMARKET TRAVELS. CAN YOU TELL POOL FIGURE IT SCHOOL OUT? I HOPE TO MEET WALRUS YOU IN SUNNY SPAIN ITALY TURKEY ISRAEL PORTUGAL.

HONDURAS
MARCH 5, 199?

ANSWERS ON THE BACK

LUNCH NOTES:

_____

_____

_____

_____

_____

_____

_____

ANSWER:

Dear Jack,

I understand from my daughter that you are trying to find me. I don't know why people named me Wrongway. There is a plan to my travels. Can you figure it out? I hope to meet you in Italy.

WRONGWAY'S TRIP SO FAR:

1. Australia
2. Brazil
3. China
4. Denmark
5. Egypt
6. France
7. Great Britain
8. Honduras
9. Italy

MEATBALL MAZE

SO FAR

Wrongway left Jack a message that there is a secret to his travel plans. Jack is on his way to Italy. Will he find him there?

I flew to Rome, Italy. I now knew there was a pattern to Wrongway's trip, but tracking him from place to place was wearing me out. I needed to figure out that pattern.

I stopped at my favorite restaurant in Rome. Over a plate of pasta, I thought things over. I don't know if it was the chewy spaghetti or the juicy meatballs that got my mind working. Suddenly everything was clear. I knew I would catch Wrongway for sure!

WHERE WILL JACK CATCH WRONGWAY? Follow each meatball with a letter in it along the spaghetti path. When you reach a blank meatball write in that letter.

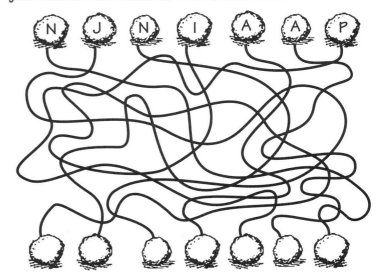

ANSWERS ON THE BACK

L U N C H   B O X   L I B R A R Y

LUNCH NOTES:

_____

_____

_____

_____

_____

_____

_____

ANSWER: In Japan

WRONGWAY'S TRIP SO FAR:

1. Australia
2. Brazil
3. China
4. Denmark
5. Egypt
6. France
7. Great Britain
8. Honduras
9. Italy
10. Japan

END OF THE LINE

SO FAR

Jack has one last stop on his search for Wrongway Faraday.

When I arrived in Japan I checked the airport time-tables. Then I went straight to gate #8. Waiting there for the flight to Kenya was Wrongway!

"Jack, old boy, great to see you!"

"Wrongway, I'm taking you home!"

He didn't seem to hear me. "I'm going on safari, Jack," he said. "I've got an extra ticket. Care to join me?"

A safari in Kenya? No world traveler would pass that up! And besides I could e-mail Leslie Faraday to say I was keeping an eye on her dad.

"Wrongway," I said. "This could be the beginning of a beautiful friendship!"

HOW DID JACK DAKOTA KNOW WRONGWAY'S NEXT DESTINATION WOULD BE KENYA? To read the answer replace each number with a letter from the alphabet. (1=a, 2=b, 3=c, etc.)

$\overline{8}$ $\overline{5}$

$\overline{23}$ $\overline{5}$ $\overline{14}$ $\overline{20}$ $\overline{9}$ $\overline{14}$

$\overline{1}$ $\overline{12}$ $\overline{16}$ $\overline{8}$ $\overline{1}$ $\overline{2}$ $\overline{5}$ $\overline{20}$ $\overline{9}$ $\overline{3}$ $\overline{1}$ $\overline{12}$

$\overline{15}$ $\overline{18}$ $\overline{4}$ $\overline{5}$ $\overline{18}$

ANSWERS ON THE BACK

LUNCH NOTES:

ANSWER: He went in alphabetical order

WRONGWAY'S TRIP:
1. Australia
2. Brazil
3. China
4. Denmark
5. Egypt
6. France
7. Great Britain
8. Honduras
9. Italy
10. Japan
11. Kenya

THE MARLOWE MIDDLE SCHOOL MYSTERY
A SCOTT LINYARD PUZZLE MYSTERY

Get ready to follow Scott Linyard through the halls and classrooms of Philip Marlowe Middle School. Help him solve the puzzles that identify the nine missing items and catch the crook.

My name is Linyard— Scott Linyard. I'm a private eye. In my business you need to be plenty tough, and I am. Only two people in the world scare me: my mother and Dr. Rhonda Stone.

That's why I was nervous when Dr. Stone, the principal at Philip Marlowe Middle School, sent for me. I entered the principal's office. Dr. Stone was older than I remembered but as strict as ever. "Be seated, Mr. Linyard," she said sternly.

"If this is about that turtle incident in 1981, I swear I don't know how it ended up in Steven Moody's gym shorts," I said.

"That was a long, long time ago," she said. "I called you because I need your help.

"Spring vacation begins next week," she continued. "I always take inventory before I close the school. Every item must be accounted for, but some prankster has hidden nine items somewhere in the school. This wise guy even removed them from my inventory list so I don't know what or where they are. Without them we cannot have our vacation! Can you find them?"

I had to chuckle at Dr. Stone's problem. After all, I like a good prank as much as the next ex-student. But I couldn't bear the thought of all those kids missing their vacation.

"Okay," I said. "I'll do it!"

KEY CLUE

DAY 1

THE PLOT

Dr. Rhonda Stone has asked Scott to identify and find nine items missing in Philip Marlowe Middle School.

I left the principal's office. I walked past rows of students grabbing books from their lockers. That's when I spotted Mallory Rogers. Nice kid, but a real pack rat. She collected everything and, from the looks of it, kept it all in her locker.

"Mind if I have a peek, Mal?" I asked.

"Be my guest," she said.

It didn't take long for my private eyes to find the first missing item!

WHAT DID SCOTT FIND? Use the clues to fill in the key words. Then write the correct letters in the message to the right.

1. Favorite Thanksgiving food:

___ ___ ___ K E Y
 1   2   3

2. A baboon is one:

___ ___ ___ K E Y
    4   5

3. Spooky door opener:

___ ___ ___ ___ ___ ___ ___ ___ K E Y
 6   7   8

4. A calculator has one:

K E Y ___ ___ ___
       9 10 11

5. Star Spangled Composer:

___ ___ ___ ___ ___ ___ ___ ___ ___ ___ K E Y
 12   13   14

                                                        ,

___ ___ ___ ___ ___   ___ ___ ___ ___ ___   ___ ___ ___ ___
 6 13 14   1   1   12 14   2   5 11   4 10   7   6

___ ___ ___ ___ ___ ___   ___ ___ ___ ___
 3   8   9 14   3   1   13 10   3 11

ANSWERS ON THE BACK

LUNCH BOX **DAY 1** LIBRARY

ANSWER:
1. Turkey
2. Monkey
3. Skeleton key
4. Keypad
5. Francis Scott Key

Scott found Mal's report card

NUMBERS, PLEASE!

DAY
· 2 ·

I hustled over to Oscar Bolero's math class. When I was in school Oscar was the class cut-up. How he ended up as a teacher is one mystery I'll never solve.

"Hello, Scotso!" he said. I hated it when he called me that.

Oscar listened while I told him about the case. "Scotso, I think I can help," he said, finally. "Some joker left me a little surprise in my desk. It must be one of the things you need."

WHAT DID OSCAR FIND? Add up the numbers in the circles. Do the same with the squares and triangles. The largest number will give you the answer.

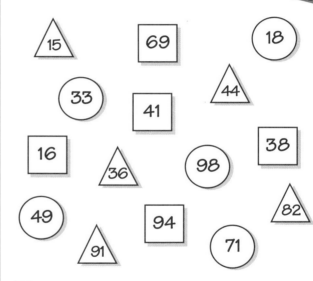

■ = A dozen dirty gym socks

▲ = A dusty chalkboard eraser

● = A slimy salamander

ANSWERS ON THE BACK

LUNCH NOTES:

_____

_____

_____

_____

_____

_____

_____

ANSWER:
■ = 258
▲ = 268
● = 269

A slimy salamander

BOOKSHELF SHUFFLE

SO FAR

Yesterday Scott found a slimy salamander in Oscar Bolero's desk. Seven items are still missing.

My next stop was a visit with Alicia Callabus—my old English teacher. As I walked into her classroom she was reading from a book to her students.

"Scott Linyard," she exclaimed. "You are just in time. Of course you remember *Johnny Tremain*?"

"I think he was in the class ahead of me," I said quickly.

Ms. C. glared at me. Her expression changed when I told her why I had come.

"Just yesterday I was looking for my copy of *Maniac Magee*," she recalled. "I noticed something odd at the very top of my bookshelves. I couldn't quite reach it, but I'm quite certain it is not a book."

I pushed a desk next to the shelves and hopped on top of it. Standing on tiptoe I was just able to reach the third missing object!

WHAT DID SCOTT FIND? Fill in each column of this puzzle to make a three-letter word. Be careful! Sometimes more than one word will fit. When you have made the correct words, the letters across will spell the missing item.

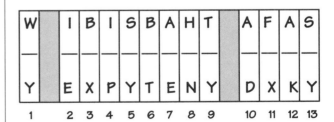

W		I	B	I	S	B	A	H	T		A	F	A	S
Y		E	X	P	Y	T	E	N	Y		D	X	K	Y
1		2	3	4	5	6	7	8	9		10	11	12	13

ANSWERS ON THE BACK

DAY 3

LUNCH BOX **DAY 3** LIBRARY

LUNCH NOTES:

ANSWER:
1. Way
2. Ice
3. Box
4. Imp
5. Spy
6. But
7. Ate
8. Hen
9. Try
10. Add
11. Fix
12. Ask
13. Sky

A computer disk

HELLO MR. CHIPS

DAY 4

SO FAR

Scott found the third missing item, a computer disk, in Ms. Callabus's English class. But where is item number four?

My next stop was the computer lab. I found Chester Chips poking at the back of one of the machines with a tiny screwdriver.

"I knew something was wrong," he said. "You'll never guess what I found messing up my hard drive."

"A bug?" I asked.

He shook his head. "A computer mouse is closer to the truth," he said. "But that's not quite it either." With that, he handed me the fourth missing item!

WHAT DID MR. CHIPS FIND? Follow this circuit maze from START to FINISH. You will find seven letters along the way. Unscramble them to find the missing item.

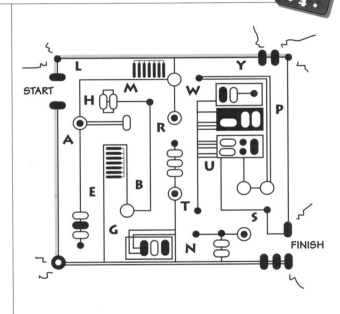

LUNCH NOTES:

_____

_____

_____

_____

_____

_____

_____

ANSWER: Hamster

MUSICAL MIX-UP

DAY
· 5 ·

SO FAR

Scott found a hamster hiding in the computer lab.

As I left the computer lab I heard a strange sound coming from down the hall. At first I didn't recognize it. Then I remembered the year I played piccolo in the Marlowe marching band. I hotfooted it over to the music room. Melody Pilot was putting her students through band practice.

The band was playing the school fight song, which sounded flatter than usual. Suddenly, I realized what the problem was. I reached into the tuba and pulled out the fifth missing item!

WHAT WAS IN THE TUBA? Unscramble the names of these six musical instruments. Then write the letters below to spell the answer.

1. MURD
   — — — —
   5   6

2. ANPOI
   — — — — —
       1 4 3

3. OOXPHNASE
   — — — — — — — — —
   11 1   4

4. METTURP
   — — — — — — —
   8 10   14

5. BOOTRMNE
   — — — — — — — —
          15   12 3

6. LOLEC
   — — — — —
   7   9

7. TRAILCEN
   — — — — — — — —
   2   13   16

— — — — — — — — — — — ,
1 2 3 4 5 6 7 8 9 10 11

— — — — —
12 13 14 15 16

ANSWERS ON THE BACK

LUNCH NOTES:

_____

_____

_____

_____

_____

_____

_____

ANSWER:
1. Drum
2. Piano
3. Saxophone
4. Trumpet
5. Trombone
6. Cello
7. Clarinet

A conductor's baton

SCOTT SCORES

DAY
· 6 ·

I stepped outside the school doors where Coach "Jumping Jack" Jeffries was giving his class a workout. The coach huffed and puffed as he led the students through their exercises.

"Glad you're on the case," he gasped. "I'm missing something and I've looked everywhere."

Just then the sun poked through the clouds. My sharp eyes spotted a shiny object hanging from the football goal posts. "No sweat, Coach," I said. "I'll take over from here."

WHAT DID SCOTT SEE? Write the correct numbers in the spaces. Then fill the bottom spaces with the matching letters from the smallest number to the largest.

1. The number of innings in a baseball game: __9__ = I

2. The number of holes on a standard golf course: ____ = T

3. The points scored when a football team makes a

   touchdown: ____ = H

4. The number of players on each team in a basketball game: ____ = W

5. The number of events in the Olympic decathlon: ____ = S

6. The highest possible score in a bowling game: ____ = E

7. The length in yards of a football field: ____ = L

__ __ __ __ __ __ __

ANSWERS ON THE BACK

LUNCH NOTES:

_____

_____

_____

_____

_____

_____

_____

ANSWER:

The numbers are

1. 9=I
2. 18=T
3. 6=H
4. 5=W
5. 10=S
6. 300=E
7. 100=L

Whistle

LEFTOVERS?

DAY
·7·

SO FAR

Scott found the coach's whistle hanging from the goal posts. There are three more items to find.

Crime-fighting works up quite an appetite. I decided to visit the school cafeteria. Hazel Parnell was behind the counter serving lunch.

"What's on the menu?" I asked, politely.

"Meat."

The meat looked the same as when I was a kid. In fact, it looked like the same piece. I passed down the line and went for the alphabet soup instead. It turned out to be a great choice. The letters in my bowl told me what I would find hidden behind the garbage can!

READ EACH SENTENCE. If it is *T R U E*, cross out the letters below. If it is *F A L S E*, go on to the next one. The leftover letters will tell you what Scott found.

1. If a whale is a mammal, cross out every A and M

2. If Charles Dickens wrote <u>Tom Sawyer</u> cross out every E and X

3. If prunes are made from plums, cross out every I and Z

4. If water boils at 212 degrees Fahrenheit at sea level cross out every G and R

```
M A A Z I M G R I Z G A A M G I R M
A M I Z G R S R R M E Z Z V I I E N
R M A I L U Z Z I R G M A N A C R H
G M I B I G Z O G X A M E R A S R I
Z I I G R M G Z Z I M A G G M A R R
```

ANSWERS ON THE BACK

LUNCH NOTES:

_____

_____

_____

_____

_____

_____

_____

ANSWER:
1. True
2. False
3. True
4. True

Seven lunch boxes

SOLAR SEARCH

DAY ·8·

SO FAR

Scott found seven lunch boxes in the school cafeteria. There are still two items missing.

After lunch I went to Clark Kerker's science lab. I could see through a crack in the door that the classroom was in total darkness. One of the first rules they teach you in detective school is to stay out of dark places. Of course they also teach you to break all the rules. I took a deep breath and stepped inside.

I found Mr. K. sticking glow-in-the-dark constellations all over the walls. By the light of the stickers, I noticed a suspicious bulge beneath the school terrarium. I lifted the tank and found another missing object!

THE NINE PLANETS ARE HIDDEN IN THIS WORD SEARCH. Circle all of them. There will be 17 letters left over. Write them in order from left to right and top to bottom to find what was missing.

```
S U N E V O Y A
U A M A T P R O
N F T U H E U M
A T L U T H C A
R P E I R N R R
U I P G A N E S
H U T S E K M Y
J N E P T U N E
```

__ ___ ____ __ ___

__ _____ __ ___

ANSWERS ON THE BACK

LUNCH NOTES:

```
S U N E V O Y A
U A M A T P R O
N F T U H E U M
A T L U T H C A
R P E I R N R R
U I P G A N E S
H U T S E K M Y
J N E P T U N E
```

ANSWER: 6. Earth
1. Saturn   7. Mars
2. Venus   8. Uranus
3. Pluto   9. Neptune
4. Mercury
5. Jupiter

A map of the night sky

SO FAR

EASY AS 1-2-3

DAY 9

The school day was nearly finished and so was this case. I was feeling pretty good until I heard shouting from the principal's office. Dr. Stone sounded madder than that time I left my Silly Putty in the movie projector.

I ran to her office and found the principal tearing through her desk. "It's gone," she groaned. "I can't find it anywhere!"

That's when I spotted something buried in her potted palm plant. There was a note, too. I read it and smiled. Not only had I recovered the final stolen item, I knew who was behind this crazy crime spree!

TO READ THE NOTE, REPLACE EACH NUMBER WITH A LETTER FROM THE ALPHABET. (1=A, 2=B, 3=C, 4=D, 5=E, ETC.) Then check Day 10 to discover "who done it."

$\overline{4}$ $\overline{5}$ $\overline{1}$ $\overline{18}$ $\overline{19}$ $\overline{3}$ $\overline{15}$ $\overline{20}$ $\overline{19}$ $\overline{15}$,

$\overline{25}$ $\overline{15}$ $\overline{21}$ $\overline{6}$ $\overline{15}$ $\overline{21}$ $\overline{14}$ $\overline{4}$ $\overline{20}$ $\overline{8}$ $\overline{5}$

$\overline{16}$ $\overline{18}$ $\overline{9}$ $\overline{14}$ $\overline{3}$ $\overline{9}$ $\overline{16}$ $\overline{1}$ $\overline{12}$

$\overline{15}$ $\overline{6}$ $\overline{20}$ $\overline{8}$ $\overline{5}$ $\overline{25}$ $\overline{5}$ $\overline{1}$ $\overline{18}$

$\overline{20}$ $\overline{18}$ $\overline{15}$ $\overline{16}$ $\overline{8}$ $\overline{25}$ $\overline{2}$ $\overline{21}$ $\overline{20}$ $\overline{25}$ $\overline{15}$ $\overline{21}$,

$\overline{23}$ $\overline{15}$ $\overline{14}$ $\overline{20}$ $\overline{6}$ $\overline{9}$ $\overline{14}$ $\overline{4}$ $\overline{13}$ $\overline{5}$!

ANSWERS ON THE BACK

LUNCH NOTES:

_____

_____

_____

_____

_____

_____

_____

ANSWER:
Dear Scotso,
You found the Principal of the Year trophy
but you won't find me!

CASE CLOSED!

DAY 10

SO FAR

Yesterday Scott found Dr. Stone's Principal of the Year trophy. Now he must find the crook!

All the missing items had been found. That left me with one last job. I wanted to turn in the prankster who had caused all this trouble. I arranged for everyone I had met to gather in the teachers' lounge.

"There's nothing I like better than a tricky crook," I began. "But the wise guy who planned this prank wasn't quite clever enough. There are fingerprints all over this school. If that wasn't enough, the final note was a dead giveaway."

With that I tapped the troublemaker on the shoulder and put an end to this school-yard caper!

WHO DID SCOTT TAP? Follow the clues. Cross out people until you are left with only one suspect. That one did it!

THE SUSPECTS:

1. The person who did it has more letters in the last name than in the first name
2. There are an odd number of letters in his or her name
3. He or she has an odd number of vowels, too
4. There are no K's in either name

ALICIA CALLABUS   JACK JEFFRIES

CHESTER CHIPS   MALLORY ROGERS

CLARK KERKER   MELODY PILOT

HAZEL PARNELL   OSCAR BOLERO

RHONDA STONE

ANSWERS ON THE BACK

LUNCH NOTES:

_____

_____

_____

_____

_____

_____

_____

ANSWER: Math teacher Oscar Bolero is the
culprit. In addition to his fingerprints,
Bolero made the mistake of calling the
detective "Scotso" in his note. Bolero is the
only person who uses that nickname.

THE GREAT ZOO ESCAPE

AN INKY O'BRIEN PUZZLE MYSTERY

My name is Inky O'Brien. I'm a reporter for the *Downtown Gazette*. I've covered some strange stories, but the wildest story of all was due to Mr. Bimps.

It started when my boss, Scoop Johnson, told me to go to the zoo and interview Mr. Bimps. He is a chimpanzee who uses sign language. After years of experiments, he had been sent to live at the zoo.

"I didn't become a reporter to interview some stupid ape!" I insisted.

"That chimp is smarter than some reporters I know," growled Scoop.

I drove over to the zoo and parked my car. As I walked in the gate, a chimp ran past me carrying a ring full of keys. I looked around and saw a leopard climbing over one fence and a rattlesnake

Join Inky O'Brien as she races around town. Solve puzzles to discover which animals she finds for her stories and help her track down Mr. Bimps.

slithering under another.

The pounding I heard was not my heart beating. Someone was banging on the door of the zoo office. I opened it and the zoo-keeper, Andy Zipper, dashed out.

"That Bimps is clever," he said. "When I turned my back on him, he locked me in my office."

"It looks as if you're about the only one he locked up," I said. "Bimps has been letting out animals left and right."

Just then an elephant thundered past us. "I've got to go" I said. "There are stories all over town and I'm going to get them!"

INN TROUBLE!

DAY 1

THE PLOT

A chimp named Mr. Bimps has turned zoo animals loose. Inky O'Brien must find the animals, including Bimps.

I had to act fast if I was going to get the scoop on the great zoo escape.

My first break came right across the street from the zoo. I saw people running out of the door of the Dewdrop Inn. Was there a connection to Bimps's monkey business?

A crowd stood out in front. I tried to talk to the manager but he was too upset to speak.

Suddenly I heard a loud crash in the lobby. I looked through the window and saw my first story!

USE THE LETTER WHEEL TO DISCOVER THE STORY.
Begin at START. Write that letter in the space below. Now count three spaces clockwise. Write the letter you find in the next space. Keep counting three spaces at a time until you have used all the letters.

START

_ _____ __

___ _____

ANSWERS ON THE BACK

LUNCH BOX **DAY 1** LIBRARY

LUNCH NOTES:

_____

_____

_____

_____

_____

_____

_____

ANSWER: A Hippo In The Hotel

SCRAMBLED BREAKFAST

DAY
· 2 ·

SO FAR

Inky found a hippo in the hotel. She must gather eight more stories and find Mr. Bimps.

Next to the hotel was Flip's Pancake Palace. It was time for the breakfast rush, but the place was nearly empty. There were plates filled with food on most of the tables. It looked as if people had left in a hurry.

I found Flip sitting alone at a booth. "Craziest thing I ever saw," he said. "My customers hopped out of their chairs as soon as he came in. And my cook? He took one look and jumped out the window!"

WHAT WAS THE PROBLEM AT FLIP'S?
Unscramble the names of these different breakfast foods. Then write the correct letters in the spaces to the right.

1. GGSE __ __ __ __
   1

2. LACERE __ __ __ __ __ __
   2   3

3. NIFUMF __ __ __ __ __ __
   4   5

4. APENKAC __ __ __ __ __ __ __
   6   7

5. SOTAT __ __ __ __ __
   8   9

6. ODUTHNUG __ __ __ __ __ __ __ __
   10 11

__ __ __ __ __ __ __ __ __ __ __
6 7 6 5 10 6 3 8 8 4 5

__ __ __ __ __ __ __ __ __ __
9 11 1 7 4 9 2 11 1 5

ANSWERS ON THE BACK

LUNCH NOTES:

_____

_____

_____

_____

_____

_____

_____

ANSWER:
1. Eggs
2. Cereal
3. Muffin
4. Pancake
5. Toast
6. Doughnut

A Kangaroo In The Kitchen

FLOWER MATCH

SO FAR

A kangaroo in the kitchen was story number two. Seven more to go!

By now word was out about the zoo animal escape. I wondered where Mr. Bimps was. Meanwhile I drove to the botanical garden. The police radio in my car said there was a disturbance in the flower beds.

Was there ever! Gardener Felix Culpepper was running through the flowers with a giant butterfly net. But that was no butterfly he was trying to catch. I giggled as I took notes for my next story.

WHAT WAS FELIX AFTER? Find the number of flowers that are a perfect match. Then check below to see what animal was loose, and where.

2 MATCHING FLOWERS = a toucan in the tulips
3 MATCHING FLOWERS = a penguin in the petunias
4 MATCHING FLOWERS = a rhea in the roses

ANSWERS ON THE BACK

LUNCH BOX DAY 3 LIBRARY

LUNCH NOTES:

_____

_____

_____

_____

_____

_____

_____

ANSWER: 3 Matching Flowers = A Penguin In The Petunias

SO FAR

Yesterday Inky found a penguin in the petunias. She is now after her fourth story.

CLUB TROUBLE

DAY
.4.

M uscle's Health Club was my next stop. A sign on the door read CLOSED. Mike Muscle blocked my path.

"Come on, Mike," I pleaded. "What's up?"

Mike would not cooperate. "I don't need no bad publicity," he explained.

I started to leave. Then I sneaked around to the side entrance and peeked through the keyhole!

WHAT DID INKY SEE INSIDE THE HEALTH CLUB? Answer the clues. Then write the letters in the spaces.

1. You hear with them: $\overline{}_{16}\ \overline{}_{1}\ \overline{}_{11}\ \overline{}_{17}$

2. Opposite of day: $\overline{}_{2}\ \overline{}_{22}\ \overline{}_{24}\ \overline{}_{15}\ \overline{}_{9}$

3. Your head rests on one at bedtime: $\overline{}_{25}\ \overline{}_{12}\ \overline{}_{4}\ \overline{}_{28}\ \overline{}_{10}\ \overline{}_{18}$

4. Jack's beanstalk enemy: $\overline{}_{7}\ \overline{}_{6}\ \overline{}_{3}\ \overline{}_{23}\ \overline{}_{14}$

5. What the post office delivers: $\overline{}_{20}\ \overline{}_{8}\ \overline{}_{19}\ \overline{}_{5}$

6. Earth's natural satellite: $\overline{}_{21}\ \overline{}_{26}\ \overline{}_{27}\ \overline{}_{13}$

$\overline{}_{1}\ \overline{}_{2}\quad \overline{}_{3}\ \overline{}_{4}\ \overline{}_{5}\ \overline{}_{6}\ \overline{}_{7}\ \overline{}_{8}\ \overline{}_{9}\ \overline{}_{10}\ \overline{}_{11}\quad \overline{}_{12}\ \overline{}_{13}$

$\overline{}_{14}\ \overline{}_{15}\ \overline{}_{16}\quad \overline{}_{17}\ \overline{}_{18}\ \overline{}_{19}\ \overline{}_{20}\ \overline{}_{21}\ \overline{}_{22}\ \overline{}_{23}\ \overline{}_{24}$

$\overline{}_{25}\ \overline{}_{26}\ \overline{}_{27}\ \overline{}_{28}$

ANSWERS ON THE BACK

LUNCH BOX **DAY 4** LIBRARY

LUNCH NOTES:

_____

_____

_____

_____

_____

_____

_____

ANSWER:
1. Ears
2. Night
3. Pillow
4. Giant
5. Mail
6. Moon

An Alligator In The Swimming Pool

ICE SCREAM!

DAY 5

SO FAR

Inky has four of the stories she needs to fill the newspaper. Here comes number five!

My next stop was Royal Roy's Ice-Cream Stand. Roy's has the hottest fudge and the hottest gossip in town. Today, however, things were different. Everyone had made like a banana and split. Things were quiet—a little too quiet.

I grabbed my notepad and camera. As I walked around Roy's on tiptoe, I scribbled notes on my pad. Suddenly I heard a growling sound. I clicked my camera and took off with another story to write!

WHAT WAS THE STORY? To find out, check Inky's notes. Write the first letters of each word in the spaces below. In order to spell the message you must go from the LAST word in Inky's note to the FIRST.

Mysterious and eerie.
Roy's customers exited.
Creatures into growling
near Inky. The animals
eat sundaes! Really are
enormous. Better retreat
and look over photos!

__ __ __ __ __   __ __ __ __   __ __ __

__ __ __   __ __ __ __

ANSWERS ON THE BACK

LUNCH BOX **DAY · 5 ·** LIBRARY

LUNCH NOTES:

_____

_____

_____

_____

_____

_____

_____

ANSWER: Polar Bears Eating Ice Cream

SQUARE ROUTE

DAY · 6 ·

SO FAR

With five stories finished, Inky has four more to go. But what about Mr. Bimps?

By now the great zoo escape was big news. I knew the prize story was finding Mr. Bimps, the chimp who started it all.

As I walked past the park, I spotted Bimps. I tried to speak to him using sign language. "Please, stop," I asked with my hands.

"Bimps go now!" was his answer. With that he turned and dashed into the park. I followed, but Bimps was too fast. I lost him.

As I turned to leave, I heard shouting from the playground. That's where I found my next story.

WHAT DID INKY SEE IN THE PLAYGROUND? Count the squares below. The exact number of squares will give you your answer.

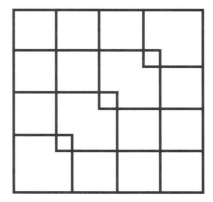

23 SQUARES = a sloth on the sliding pond
25 SQUARES = an orangutan on the monkey bars
27 SQUARES = a camel in the sandbox

ANSWERS ON THE BACK

LUNCH NOTES:

22

4	5	6	7
8	9	10 [1]	11
12	13 [2]	14	15
16	17 [3]	18	19

20

23

21

24

25

26: Square Made Out Of 9, 10, 13, 14, 1, 2, 3
27: The Whole Square

ANSWER: A Camel In The Sandbox

A CAT-TASTROPHE!

DAY · 7 ·

SO FAR

Inky found a camel in the sandbox. She must find three more stories and Mr. Bimps.

I decided to check out the Explorers Club. Long ago big game hunters gathered there to talk about safaris.

Club president Teddy Kessler met me on the steps of the building. "I wouldn't go inside," he warned.

"Is it still men only?" I asked.

"Actually we have a female guest today," he said. Teddy showed me a snapshot of the animal inside.

WHAT IS WAITING INSIDE? Fill in the CAT words. Then write the correct letters in the spaces to the right.

1. It turns into a butterfly:
   C A T __ __ __ __ __ __ __
            1   2 3

2. A herd of steers:
   C A T __ __ __
           4   5

3. A book for ordering things by mail:
   C A T __ __ __ __
               6 7

4. Also spelled ketchup:
   C A T __ __ __
           8 9

5. A popular girl's name:
   C A T __ __ __ __ __ __
           10   11

__ __ __ __ __ __ __ __ __ __ __ __ __
3 2 1 6 11 5 8 8 1 11 4 10 5

__ __ __ __ __ __
2 6 9 11 7 5

ANSWERS ON THE BACK

LUNCH NOTES:

_____

_____

_____

_____

_____

_____

_____

ANSWER:
1. Caterpillar
2. Cattle
3. Catalog
4. Catsup
5. Catherine

A Lioness In The Lounge

GOING UP

SO FAR

Inky needs two more stories. Will she also find Mr. Bimps?

I decided to check out the town from the top of its tallest building. So I went to Bump Tower. From the top of the skyscraper I spotted pandas in the park, moose at the mall and hyenas on the highway. As I took notes, I heard someone shouting, "Everyone out at once!"

I turned around to see Ronald Bump.

"Is King Kong coming up here?" I asked.

"Never mind the wisecracks," said Bump. "Just leave. And be sure to take the stairs!"

WHAT WAS IN BUMP TOWER? To find out, replace each letter below the dashes with the one that appears next to it in the skyscraper.

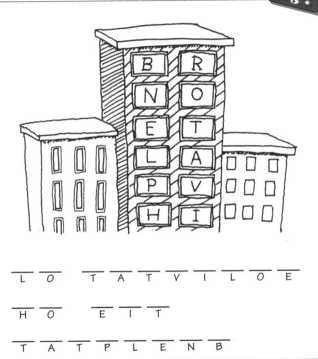

B R
N O
E T
L A
P V
H I

L O T A T V I L O E

H O E I T

T A T P L E N B

LUNCH BOX DAY · 8 · LIBRARY

LUNCH NOTES:

_____

_____

_____

_____

_____

_____

_____

ANSWER: An Elephant In The Elevator

MONKEY BUSINESS

DAY
· 9 ·

SO FAR

Inky needs to get one more story for her paper and to find out what's wrong with Mr. Bimps.

I went back to the zoo to see how things were going. The zookeeper, Andy Zipper, stopped me just outside the parking lot. He looked exhausted, but happy.

"We've got almost all the animals back," he said.

"What about Mr. Bimps?" I asked.

"Still missing," said Zipper, "but we're about to collect his best buddy."

I joined Andy in a zoo jeep and we drove to a nearby shopping center. While I watched, the zoo crew coaxed another animal into their wagon.

WHAT ANIMAL DID THEY FIND? Fill in the spaces using the names of the animals Inky has found so far. The first number under the space tells you which animal to check. The second number tells you which letter to use. The first one is filled in to get you started.

1. ALLIGATOR
2. CAMEL
3. ELEPHANT
4. HIPPO
5. KANGAROO
6. LIONESS
7. PENGUIN
8. POLAR BEAR

A
‾‾‾ ‾‾‾ ‾‾‾ ‾‾‾ ‾‾‾ ‾‾‾ ‾‾‾ ‾‾‾   ‾‾‾ ‾‾‾
1-1 1-5 1-8 5-6 4-2 6-1 3-2 2-2   7-6 6-4

‾‾‾ ‾‾‾ ‾‾‾   ‾‾‾ ‾‾‾ ‾‾‾ ‾‾‾ ‾‾‾ ‾‾‾
1-7 4-1 2-4   5-4 8-4 1-9 8-8 1-5 7-2

ANSWERS ON THE BACK

LUNCH BOX **DAY 9** LIBRARY

LUNCH NOTES:

_____

_____

_____

_____

_____

_____

_____

ANSWER: A Gorilla In The Garage

HAND TO HAND

DAY 10

SO FAR

Inky has her nine stories. But what about Mr. Bimps, the chimp who started it all?

The great zoo escape was nearly over. I needed to get to the office to finish writing my stories. As I returned to my car, I saw someone inside reading a road map. It was Bimps!

Using sign language, I interviewed him. "You are supposed to be smart," I signed. "Why did you do it?"

"Not my fault," he replied.

"I don't understand," I said. "The zoo is your new home. Why cause trouble?"

I watched Bimps's hands as they spelled out an answer. Finally I understood what was wrong. "I don't know if I can help you," I said. "But I will promise to try."

The chimp looked at me, and I swear he smiled!

WHAT WAS MR. BIMPS'S PROBLEM? Use the hand alphabet code to find the answer.

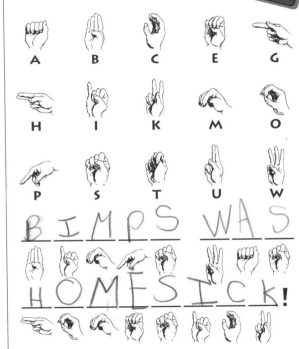

ANSWERS ON THE BACK

LUNCH BOX DAY 10 LIBRARY

LUNCH NOTES:

_____

_____

_____

_____

_____

_____

_____

ANSWER:
Bimps was homesick

LOOK OUT FOR LANDMARKS

A JACK DAKOTA PUZZLE MYSTERY

My name is Jack Dakota and I love adventure. I've wrestled crocodiles and hung by my fingernails from icy cliffs. So why am I afraid of Snapper?

This particular Snapper is not a turtle. It's Violet "Snapper" Collins, world traveler and photographer.

The other day I was catching up on my paperwork. Suddenly my office door flew open and Snapper walked in.

"Hello, Violet," I said coolly.

"Jack, you just stapled your shirt to the desk," she answered with a sly grin.

"I meant to do that!" I said, lamely.

> Join Jack Dakota and Snapper Collins as they travel across America. Identify nine famous landmarks and help Snapper win the Golden Flashbulb Award.

"No time for small talk, Jack. We have work to do! Two weeks from tonight is the annual Golden Flashbulb Award. This year I'm nominated for my pictures of famous monuments. Unfortunately, my cat, Tiger, kicked over a glass of root beer, ruining nine of my best negatives. I have to shoot new photos of those landmarks right away!"

"I'm sure you can do this without me."

"That's true, but it wouldn't be as much fun," she said with a smile. "Of course if you have too much paperwork…"

I thought it over. Things could get pretty wild when Snapper was around. On the other hand they were never boring.

"Okay," I said, finally. "Let's go."

INCH BY INCH

DAY 1

THE PLOT

Jack Dakota and Violet "Snapper" Collins must photograph nine U.S. landmarks. Which one will be first?

Snapper and I started our adventure in New York City. We needed a helicopter so I looked up Charlie Johnson. Charlie and I once flew a glider across the Grand Canyon. Now he was known as "Chopper Chuck." He flew a news helicopter over traffic jams.

Chopper Chuck, Snapper and I took off for a bird's-eye view of the Big Apple. I turned to say something to Snapper, but she wasn't there. She was hanging out of the door, upside down from the helicopter!

"Can't talk now!" she shouted over the roar of the copter blades. "I have work to do!"

WHAT DID SNAPPER PHOTOGRAPH? It is the famous New York landmark that is exactly 15,000 inches tall. Change inches to feet to find the answer.

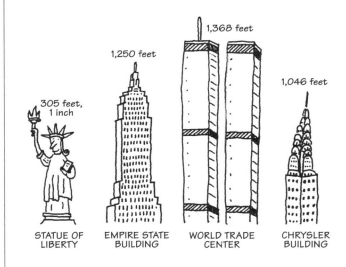

305 feet, 1 inch
STATUE OF LIBERTY

1,250 feet
EMPIRE STATE BUILDING

1,368 feet
WORLD TRADE CENTER

1,046 feet
CHRYSLER BUILDING

ANSWERS ON THE BACK

LUNCH BOX **DAY** **·1·** LIBRARY

LUNCH NOTES:

_____

_____

_____

_____

_____

_____

_____

ANSWER: The Empire State Building

BASEBALL JUMBLE

LUNCH BOX LIBRARY

SO FAR

Jack Dakota helped Snapper Collins get a picture of the Empire State Building. What will she photograph next?

Snapper and I caught the next train out of town. As I put her bags on the rack above my seat, a baseball rolled out of one bag and conked me right on the head.

"Ouch!" I groaned.

"Nice catch," Snapper laughed.

As usual Snapper had an explanation. Her next photograph would be a picture of a famous ballpark. She figured she might as well get some autographs too!

WHICH BALLPARK IS IT? Unscramble the names of these four baseball teams. Then write the letters below to spell to answer.

1. TAALTAN VRESBA

___ ___ ___ ___ ___ ___ ___   ___ ___ ___ ___ ___ ___
   1   2   3

2. SANKAS YTCI YOASLR

___ ___ ___ ___ ___ ___   ___ ___ ___ ___ ___ ___ ___
        4   5   6   7

3. DELLNAVCE DINNSIA

___ ___ ___ ___ ___ ___ ___ ___ ___   ___ ___ ___ ___ ___ ___
 8   9   10   11

4. ADLOFRI ANSMILR

___ ___ ___ ___ ___ ___ ___   ___ ___ ___ ___ ___ ___ ___
        12   13   14

___ ___ ___ ___ ___ ___   ___ ___ ___ ___ ___   ___ ___
 8 11 13 10   9   4   5 11 12 10   3   14   4

___ ___ ___ ___ ___ ___ ___ ___ ___
 2 11   7   1 14 13   6 12   9

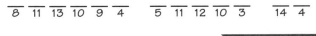

ANSWERS ON THE BACK

LUNCH BOX **DAY 2** LIBRARY

LUNCH NOTES:

_____

_____

_____

_____

_____

_____

_____

ANSWER:
1. Atlanta Braves
2. Kansas City Royals
3. Cleveland Indians
4. Florida Marlins

Camden Yards in Baltimore

WRONG NUMBER?

DAY 3

SO FAR

Jack and Snapper photographed Camden Yards in Baltimore. They must now get to landmark number three.

The baseball game between the Orioles and the Yankees went into extra innings. We stayed until the Yankees won and then went on to Washington, D.C. When we arrived in Union Station it was midnight.

I went to a phone booth to call for a taxi. While I waited, I heard Snapper mumble something about taking a photo and seeing an old friend.

The operator told me to deposit 25 cents for the first four minutes. I turned to ask Snapper for a quarter but she had disappeared!

"That's typical," I growled. Just then I noticed a strange note pinned to the phone booth door!

WHAT DID THE NOTE SAY? Use this phone code to find the answer. Replace each number in the message with one of the three letters that goes with it on a telephone. A few letters are already filled in.

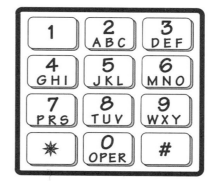

1	2 ABC	3 DEF
4 GHI	5 JKL	6 MNO
7 PRS	8 TUV	9 WXY
✳	0 OPER	#

I   _   _   G   O   _   _   _   _   _   _
4   2   6   4   6   4   6   4   8   6

_   _   _   W   H   _   _   _   _   _   _   _
8   4   3   9   4   4   8   3   4   6   8   7   3

ANSWERS ON THE BACK

LUNCH BOX **DAY 3** LIBRARY

LUNCH NOTES:

_____

_____

_____

_____

_____

_____

_____

ANSWER: I am going to the White House

WINDOW WORDS

SO FAR
—
Snapper took a photograph of the White House. Now she and Jack must get picture four.

DAY 4

Snapper and I flew to Chicago, Illinois. I was still steamed about what happened in Washington.

"You know, I would have liked to have met the President at the White House," I said for the tenth time.

"Stop grumbling about it, Jack," was Snapper's reply. "We got the photo, didn't we?"

In Chicago I did meet a president. My old friend Wanda Snow was president of Ajax Window Washers. Wanda had given me my first job washing windows at the Bon Voyage Travel Center.

Wanda set up a window-washing platform for us. As she hoisted us up the side of a building, Snapper got her fourth picture.

WHAT DID SNAPPER SHOOT? Fill in the boxes with letters to make words that read across. Be careful—sometimes more than one letter will work. Reading down, the correct letters spell the name of a famous landmark in Chicago.

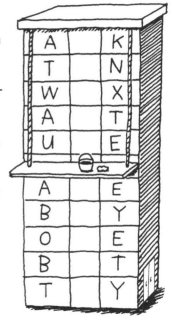

A		K
T		N
W		X
A		T
U		E

A		E
B		Y
O		E
B		T
T		Y

ANSWERS ON THE BACK

LUNCH BOX **DAY 4** LIBRARY

LUNCH NOTES:

_____

_____

_____

_____

_____

_____

_____

ANSWER:
1. Ask
2. Ten
3. Wax
4. Art
5. Use
6. Ate
7. Boy
8. Owe
9. Bet
10. Try

Sears Tower

PADDLE POWER

SO FAR

Jack and Snapper got a picture of Chicago's Sears Tower. That's four down and five to go.

Traveling with Snapper made me jumpier than a jackrabbit. I needed to relax. I got my chance when we took a steamboat down the Mississippi River. A trip on water always calms my nerves. Snapper, however, was not a happy camper. As soon as we hit the water she turned seasick green. She spent most of the trip hanging over the steamboat rail.

Before long we floated past another city and landmark. Snapper was still too queasy to notice, so I grabbed the camera and took the picture for her!

WHAT DID JACK SEE? Use the clues to fill in the words. Then match the letters to the numbers below.

1. You hang one over a window: __ __ __ __ __ __ __
   10 21 9 3 2 12 13

2. This plus wind moves a boat: __ __ __ __
   14 6 16 19

3. Happy dogs do this with their tails: __ __ __
   5 8 1

4. Opposite of quiet: __ __ __ __ __
   17 20 22 23 7

5. A furnace produces lots of this: __ __ __ __
   11 4 15 18

__ __ __ __ __ __ __   __ __ __ __
1 2 3 4 5 6 7   8 9 10 11

__ __   __ __ __ __ __
12 13   14 15 16 17 18

__ __ __ __ __
19 20 21 22 23

ANSWERS ON THE BACK

LUNCH NOTES:

ANSWER:
1. Curtain
2. Sail
3. Wag
4. Noisy
5. Heat

Gateway Arch in Saint Louis

FRISCO FIND

DAY 6

SO FAR

Jack took a photo of Gateway Arch in Saint Louis. Now he and Snapper are after picture number six.

After our trip down the Mississippi River we went west. Our plane was late (and so were we) when we reached San Francisco. As we checked into our hotel I said good night to Snapper and went to my room.

I woke in the morning, and stumbled downstairs for breakfast. I asked the waiter where Snapper was. "She disappeared into the morning fog an hour ago," he explained. "But she said if a handsome adventurer should come down for breakfast to give him this note!"

TO READ SNAPPER'S NOTE UNSCRAMBLE THE WORDS IN CAPITAL LETTERS.

RADE Jack,

Boy, are you a PEELSY head. I bet a California QUARKATHEE wouldn't wake you! I wanted to KEAT a CUETRIP in the early morning GFO. First I will DERI a BLECA RAC. Then I will take a HOTOP of the DOGNEL TEGA GREDIB.

—Snapper

ANSWERS ON THE BACK

LUNCH NOTES:

_____

_____

_____

_____

_____

_____

_____

ANSWER:

Dear Jack,

Boy, are you a sleepy head. I bet a California earthquake wouldn't wake you! I
wanted to take a picture in the early morning fog. First I will ride a cable car.
Then I will take a photo of the Golden Gate Bridge.

—Snapper

PLANE DRAIN

DAY 7

SO FAR

The sixth photo was of the Golden Gate Bridge. Three to go for Jack and Snapper.

Leona Swallow and I used to fly paper airplanes together in elementary school. Now she had a thriving seaplane business in San Francisco.

Leona loaned us a pair of wings and we flew north. Snapper insisted on being the pilot. She said I flew too slowly. I could fly rings around her, but I decided to relax and enjoy the ride.

Big mistake. As we reached Puget Sound, Snapper turned toward the next landmark. (Instead of taking a picture, she flew right at it.)

Then I noticed that look in her eye. The last time I had seen it she had been lens cap to nose with a charging rhino. I held my breath. As we buzzed the landmark, Snapper shot the perfect picture!

WHAT WAS THE LANDMARK? To decode the answer you must do three things:

1. Cross out all letters that appear in the word BURY

2. Change each X to an E

3. When you are done, read the five words from bottom to top

WARBYSHURINYGURTOBYN

SXATUTLXY

BRINY

NXUXYDLX

SPRACUX

ANSWERS ON THE BACK

LUNCH BOX **DAY 7** LIBRARY

LUNCH NOTES:

_____

_____

_____

_____

_____

_____

_____

ANSWER: Space Needle in Seattle, Washington

LA MAZE

SO FAR

Space Needle in Seattle was the seventh landmark. Two more to go for Jack and Snapper!

DAY 8

We turned our plane south and flew to Los Angeles. As soon as we landed I reached into my jacket for my coolest pair of shades. Snapper was busy, too. She was lacing up a pair of roller blades.

"You really ought to wear knee pads if you…"

"Thanks for the warning, Mom," laughed Snapper as she raced down the street.

Just then a kid came by on his mountain bike. I flagged him down and the two of us took off after her!

WHERE IS SNAPPER GOING? Follow the maze to see which landmark it leads to.

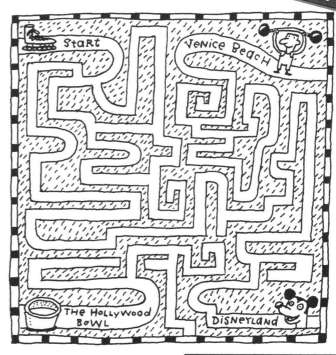

ANSWERS ON THE BACK

LUNCH BOX DAY · 8 · LIBRARY

LUNCH NOTES:

_____

_____

_____

_____

_____

_____

_____

ONE MORE SEARCH

LUNCH BOX LIBRARY

SO FAR

Disneyland was famous place number eight. One more to go.

The Golden Flashbulb Award ceremony was tomorrow. "Well, Snapper," I said. "We'd better hurry if we're going to get back in time…"

"No can do, Jack," chirped Snapper. "We've got one more stop on the way back." Another stop? "Snapper, I'm exhausted and practically out of money."

"Don't get lazy on me now, Jack," she said. "One more photo and I'm sure to win that award!"

LOOK AT THE LIST OF FAMOUS PLACES THAT SNAPPER AND JACK HAVE VISITED. Many names are misspelled. Write the INCORRECT letters in order in the spaces below to spell the last place they will visit. (Hint: Some words have two wrong letters.)

1. SPACE MEEDLE
2. OAMDEN YURDS
3. ENTIRE STATE BUILDING
4. WHITE HORSE
5. GATEWAY URCH
6. GOLDEN GASH BRIDGE
7. SEAMS TOWOR
8. DISNEYLARE

— — — — —

— — — — — — — —

ANSWERS ON THE BACK

LUNCH BOX **DAY · 9 ·** LIBRARY

ANSWER:
1. Space Ⓜeedle
2. Ⓞamden YⓊrds
3. EⓃⓉire State Building
4. White HoⓇse
5. Gateway Ⓤrch
6. Golden GaⓈⒽ Bridge
7. SeaⓂs TowⓄr
8. DisneylaⓇⒺ

Mount Rushmore

END OF THE LINE

DAY 10

SO FAR

Mount Rushmore was the final photo. But did Snapper Collins win the Golden Flashbulb Award?

We arrived back in town the morning of the award. I dropped Snapper at the photo lab. Then I raced home to get my tuxedo out of mothballs.

We met that night at the ceremony. Snapper was cool, calm and confident "Do you think you'll win?" I asked her.

She gave me one of her you've-got-to-be-kidding looks. That's Snapper for you. I just sighed and sat back in my seat.

I wasn't surprised when they announced Snapper's name for the award, or when she gave me a hug and raced to the stage to get it. But when they flashed the winning picture on their giant screen I started grinning from ear to ear. For once I had the last laugh on old Snapper!

WHY WAS JACK DAKOTA HAPPY? The answer is hidden below. The letters in each word are backwards. To read the message, first turn around the letters in each word. For example, the first word "reppans" is "Snapper."

REPPANS NOW EHT NEDLOG

BLUBHSALF DRAWA ROF REH

HPARGOTOHP FO YAWETAG HCRA.

TAHT SI EHT ENO ERUTCIP EHS DID

TON EKAT FLESREH. KCAJ KOOT TI.

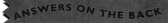
ANSWERS ON THE BACK

LUNCH NOTES:

_____

_____

_____

_____

_____

_____

_____

ANSWER: Snapper won the Golden Flashbulb Award
for her photograph of Gateway Arch. That is the one
picture she did not take herself. Jack took it.

THE MYSTERY AT THE MALL
A SCOTT LINYARD PUZZLE MYSTERY

Follow Scott Linyard as he searches the mall for Malcolm Frisby. Solve puzzles that will help him crack this case.

My name is Linyard—Scott Linyard. I'm a private eye. In detective school they said we would spend our days sneaking down dark alleys and deserted streets. I guess that's true most days, but not on Saturday. That's when I head for the mall.

I was sitting at my regular table at Cocoa Loco's, sipping a double hot chocolate and waiting for my buddy Malcolm Frisby. Malcolm is the owner of one of the mall's most popular stores. It's called The Practical Joker. If you need an ice cube with a fake bug in it or a whoopee cushion, that's the place to go. Today Malcom was nowhere in sight.

I decided to check the office for messages. I punched in the number on my cell phone and listened. There were three messages from my mother and one from someone who sounded out of breath and excited. It was Malcolm!

"Scott, I need your help right away. I was over at the store when I saw something strange happening in the mall. I'm going to look around until I find out exactly what . . ."

There was a click and the message stopped suddenly. Was Malcolm in trouble? What was happening at the mall that worried him? I paid my check and hurried out the door. I had work to do!

TRICKY LIST

THE PLOT

Scott Linyard is on a new case. He must find his friend Malcolm Frisby who has disappeared somewhere at the mall.

My first stop was The Practical Joker. The store manager, Pauline Waters, was arranging a display of rainbow-colored wigs in the window.

"Good to see you, Scott," she said. "Malcolm thought you might stop by. He left a few minutes ago in a big hurry."

"Did he say anything?"

"He told me to give you this." Pauline handed me a slip of paper. "It's Malcolm's errand list. Follow it and you're sure to find him somewhere."

"But this list is in code," I said.

"That's Malcolm for you," she said with a chuckle.

HELP SCOTT CRACK THE CODE. The letters in each word are written backwards. The first two words are done to get you started.

1. TUP RIA NI EHT ERAPS   <u>PUT AIR</u>

2. PEEK YM GIW MRAW   _____

3. TEG ETAMYALP ROF YLLOP   _____

4. XIF YM KCOTKCIT   _____

5. KCIP PU YCNAF STNAP   _____

6. TEG SMUM ROF MOM   _____

7. YUB NUF SRETAOLF   _____

8. EKAT EHT EKAC   _____

ANSWERS ON THE BACK

LUNCH NOTES:

_____

_____

_____

_____

_____

_____

_____

ANSWER:
1. Put air in the spare
2. Keep my wig warm
3. Get playmate for Polly
4. Fix my ticktock
5. Pick up fancy pants
6. Get mums for Mom
7. Buy fun floaters
8. Take the cake

CAR CALCULATIONS

DAY 2

SO FAR

Yesterday Scott found a list of places in the mall where Malcolm Frisby might be. Now he must visit them in order.

The first errand on Malcolm's list was to "put air in the spare." I hustled over to Otto's Auto-rama. If I hurried maybe I could catch up with Malcolm.

"You just missed him," Otto said when I asked about Malcolm. "Frisby paid for a new spare tire, but he said to give it to you to put in his car. It's the one in the parking lot with 'MF' on the license plate."

Me put away the spare? That made about as much sense as wearing a raincoat in the Sahara Desert. But I had no other leads, so I rolled the tire out to the parking lot. That's when I discovered six cars that could belong to Malcolm Frisby!

HELP SCOTT FIND THE CORRECT CAR. It is the only one with a number that can be evenly divided by every number from 1 through 9.

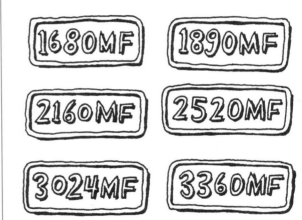

1680MF   1890MF

2160MF   2520MF

3024MF   3360MF

ANSWERS ON THE BACK

LUNCH BOX DAY 2 LIBRARY

LUNCH NOTES:

_____

_____

_____

_____

_____

_____

_____

HAT TRICK

DAY · 3 ·

L U N C H B O X   L I B R A R Y

SO FAR

Scott put a spare tire in Malcolm Frisby's car with the license plate 2520 MF. But where is his friend?

The next errand listed was to "keep my wig warm." Malcolm needed a hat. Unfortunately no one had seen him at the Bonnet Boutique or the Beanie Barn. Then I remembered that Malcolm loved baseball caps. I knew where to find those at the mall.

"Sure, I've seen him," said Dan, the owner of Dan's Dugout Duds. "He bought two caps—one for him and one for you."

Dan handed me the cap. As I tried it on, I smiled. Leave it to Malcolm to remember my favorite sports team.

WHAT SPORTS CAP WAS IT? Fill in the cities that go with each of the teams below. Then read the first letters down to spell the name of Scott's favorite team.

1. ☐_____ Indians (baseball)
2. ☐_____ Rockets (basketball)
3. ☐_____ Colts (football)
4. ☐_____ Cavaliers (basketball)
5. ☐_____ Braves (baseball)
6. ☐_____ Packers (football)
7. ☐_____ Magic (basketball)
8. ☐_____ Red Sox (baseball)
9. ☐_____ Jazz (basketball)
10. ☐_____ Lakers (basketball)
11. ☐_____ Dodgers (baseball)
12. ☐_____ Spurs (basketball)

ANSWERS ON THE BACK

LUNCH NOTES:

ANSWER:
1. Cleveland Indians
2. Houston Rockets
3. Indianapolis Colts
4. Cleveland Cavaliers
5. Atlanta Braves
6. Green Bay Packers
7. Orlando Magic
8. Boston Red Sox
9. Utah Jazz
10. Los Angeles Lakers
11. Los Angeles Dodgers
12. San Antonio Spurs

Chicago Bulls

PET PUZZLE

DAY · 4 ·

SO FAR

Yesterday Scott picked up a Chicago Bulls cap. He must look for Malcolm Frisby in six more places.

Malcolm next planned to "get playmate for Polly." I knew that Polly was Malcolm's pet parakeet, so I hustled over to Pets Etc. where my old friend Carlotta Furball was waiting. I explained why I had come and asked if Malcolm had left a parakeet for me.

"Oh, he left something for you," laughed Carlotta. She handed me a long box. "But it's no parakeet!"

WHAT WAS IN THE BOX? Use the clues to fill in the words. Then match the letters with the numbers to the right.

1. A ghost's favorite word: $\overline{}\ \overline{}\ \overline{}$
   $\quad\quad 12\ \ 9\ \ 10$

2. Tigers and lions: $\overline{}\ \overline{}\ \overline{}\ \overline{}$
   $\quad\quad 15\ \ 1\ \ 23\ \ 18$

3. A drying cloth: $\overline{}\ \overline{}\ \overline{}\ \overline{}\ \overline{}$
   $\quad\quad 19\ \ 13\ \ 3\ \ 4\ \ 5$

4. Word for ½ or ⅔: $\overline{}\ \overline{}\ \overline{}\ \overline{}\ \overline{}\ \overline{}\ \overline{}\ \overline{}$
   $\quad\quad 8\ \ 20\ \ 14\ \ 22\ \ 11\ \ 21\ \ 16\ \ 17$

5. Person who casts a ballot: $\overline{}\ \overline{}\ \overline{}\ \overline{}\ \overline{}$
   $\quad\quad 6\ \ 24\ \ 2\ \ 7\ \ 25$

$\overline{\ 1\ }\quad \overline{\ 2\ }\ \overline{\ 3\ }\ \overline{\ 4\ }\ \overline{\ 5\ }\ \overline{\ 6\ }\ \overline{\ 7\ }\text{-}$

$\overline{\ 8\ }\ \overline{\ 9\ }\ \overline{10}\ \overline{11}\qquad \overline{12}\ \overline{13}\ \overline{14}$

$\overline{15}\ \overline{16}\ \overline{17}\ \overline{18}\ \overline{19}\ \overline{20}\ \overline{21}\ \overline{22}\ \overline{23}\ \overline{24}\ \overline{25}$

ANSWERS ON THE BACK

LUNCH NOTES:

_____

_____

_____

_____

_____

_____

_____

ANSWER:
1. Boo
2. Cats
3. Towel
4. Fraction
5. Voter

A twelve-foot boa constrictor

WHICH WATCH?

DAY
· 5 ·

SO FAR

Scott picked up a boa constrictor at Pets Etc. He must look for Malcolm Frisby in five more places.

The next errand on his list was to "fix my ticktock." At the mall a busted timepiece meant a visit to Grandpa's Clock Shop. I found Grandpa fixing a cuckoo clock. I told him I was searching for Malcolm.

"Cuckoo!"

"I know he is," I replied. "But I need to find him."

"You're too late," said Grandpa. "Malcolm left in such a hurry he forgot to take his timepiece. You had better take it with you when you go."

WHICH CLOCK WAS MALCOLM'S? Answer each question T R U E or F A L S E. Use the number of T R U E answers to find the correct timepiece.

1. A mile is longer than a kilometer: (TRUE OR FALSE?)
2. A trapezoid has four sides: (TRUE OR FALSE?)
3. All spiders have eight legs: (TRUE OR FALSE?)
4. Kangaroos live in Austria: (TRUE OR FALSE?)
5. Ostriches cannot fly: (TRUE OR FALSE?)
6. Penguins live near the North Pole and South Pole: (TRUE OR FALSE?)
7. Saturn is the largest planet in the solar system: (TRUE OR FALSE?)
8. There are 32 fluid ounces in a quart: (TRUE OR FALSE?)
9. There are seven continents on Earth: (TRUE OR FALSE?)
10. Leap year comes every three years: (TRUE OR FALSE?)

4 TRUE = a grandfather clock
5 TRUE = an alarm clock
6 TRUE = a stopwatch

ANSWERS ON THE BACK

LUNCH BOX **DAY 5** LIBRARY

LUNCH NOTES:

ANSWER:
1. True
2. True
3. True
4. False
5. True
6. False
7. False
8. True
9. True
10. False

There are six true answers: Scott picked a stopwatch

SO FAR

Yesterday Scott found Malcolm's stopwatch. He has four more chances to find Malcolm.

DOUBLE TROUBLE

DAY · 6

When I began looking for Malcolm Frisby I was worried. Now I was just plain angry. I was tired of his silly errands. But at detective school they teach you to finish the job. The next item on the list was "pick up fancy pants," so I scrambled over to Tuxedo Junction.

The clerk filled me in. "Frisby was just here to pick up his tuxedo . . ."

I had to interrupt. "But he left it for me, right?"

"Nope, he took it," the clerk continued, "but he forgot to take these!"

WHAT DID MALCOLM LEAVE FOR SCOTT THIS TIME? Unscramble each word at right. (Hint: Each word has double letters somewhere in it.)

1. SSRAG   _____
2. UUVACM   _____
3. SSEDR   _____
4. PPEAL   _____
5. EEESCH   _____
6. NNYUF   _____
7. DDRELA   _____
8. EEERRZF   _____
9. RROOOWMT   _____
10. SSDDEER   _____

Now write the double letters from 1 to 10 to spell the word. You should write only one of the letters each time.

__ __ __ __ __ __ __ __ __ __

ANSWERS ON THE BACK

LUNCH NOTES:

ANSWER:
1. Grass
2. Vacuum
3. Dress
4. Apple
5. Cheese
6. Funny
7. Ladder
8. Freezer
9. Tomorrow
10. Dressed

Suspenders

FLOWER SEARCH

DAY · 7 ·

L U N C H B O X L I B R A R Y

Malcolm Frisby's next errand was to "get mums for Mom." I scooted over to Fawn's Floral Warehouse. As I stepped through the door I was surrounded by the sweet smell of flowers.

I found Fawn in the back of the shop repotting her petunias. I filled her in.

"He bought all my chrysanthemums," Fawn said. "And when he saw what was growing in my hothouse he said that that was the plant for you!"

WHAT PLANT WAS IT? Circle the 11 flowers hidden in this word search. There will be 13 letters left over. Write them in order from left to right and top to bottom to find your answer.

CARNATION   MARIGOLD   POPPY
DAFFODIL   PANSY   ROSE
DAISY   VIOLET   LILY
LAVENDER   TULIP

```
D C A V P E V N
D A F F O D I L
L R I U P R O A
O N L S P O L V
G A T I Y S E E
I T S U L E T N
R I F L L Y Y D
A O T R A I P E
M N Y S N A P R
```

_ _ _ _ _ _ _ , _ _ _ _ _ _

ANSWERS ON THE BACK

LUNCH NOTES:

_____

_____

_____

_____

_____

_____

_____

```
O C A V P E V N
D A F F O D I L
L R I U P R O A
O N L S P O L V
G A T I S E E
I T S U L E T N
R I F L L Y Y D
A O T R A I P E
M N Y S N A P R
```

ANSWER: A Venus' flytrap

MINUS MIME

DAY
· 8 ·

SO FAR

Yesterday Scott picked up a Venus' flytrap. He has two errands left in his search for Malcolm Frisby.

Until now I had been able to figure out the items on Malcolm's list. But "buy fun floaters" had me flustered. Just then I spotted a clown handing out balloons. As I walked over I decided to get tough.

"Okay, what's with the floaters?" I demanded.

Honk!

"Don't get smart with me, Bozo," I growled. "I want answers and I want them now."

He handed me a card. I recognized Malcolm Frisby's squiggly writing. "Scott," it read. "Please grab a batch of balloons. Not too few nor too many, okay?"

WORK FROM BOTTOM TO TOP TO FILL IN ALL THE NUMBERS. Take the balloons that are side-by-side. Subtract the smaller number from the larger one. Write the answer in the balloon above the pair. Keep subtracting pairs until you reach the top balloon. The top balloon shows the number Scott needs.

ANSWERS ON THE BACK

LUNCH NOTES:

ANSWER:

16

65   49

385   450   401

549   164   614   213

A CRUMBY CLUE!

DAY 9

SO FAR

The clown at the mall gave Scott 16 balloons. There is one place left to visit. Will Malcolm Frisby be there?

The last item on the list was "take the cake." I followed the smell of baking brownies over to Pablo's Pastry Palace.

"Malcolm was here, but you missed him," said Pablo.

"I had a funny feeling you would say that," I replied.

Pablo reached behind the counter and handed me a cardboard box. I looked inside and broke into a smile. At last I knew what was going on. And I knew where to find Malcolm Frisby, too!

WHAT WAS IN THE BOX? Fill in the spaces to find out. The first number under the space tells you which bakery item to check. The second number tells you which letter in that line to use. The first few are filled in to get you started.

1. PEACH PIE
2. BANANA WALNUT MUFFIN
3. CHOCOLATE COOKIES
4. DATE NUT BREAD

<u>A</u> <u>P</u> <u>I</u> __ __ __ __ __ __ __
1-3   1-1 1-7 2-3 1-8 2-2 1-1 1-6 3-6 4-10

__ __ __ __ __ __ - __ __ __ __
2-11 1-1 3-16 1-7 4-12 4-4   4-1 3-3 2-7 4-5

__ __ __ __
3-10 3-7 3-13 1-8

ANSWERS ON THE BACK

LUNCH NOTES:

_____

_____

_____

_____

_____

_____

_____

ANSWER: A pineapple upside-down cake.

CASE CLOSED!

DAY · 10

SO FAR

Scott picked up a pineapple upside-down cake. Now all that is left is to find Malcolm Frisby.

My journey through the mall was nearly over. I thought about Frisby's odd errand list. If I hadn't been worried about my friend I might have caught on sooner.

I went back to where it all began. I stepped through the door at Cocoa Loco's and walked to my regular table. Malcolm was there wearing a tuxedo and a smile. He handed me a card.

I read it. "Thanks a lot, my friend," I said finally. "It was worth the trip." We ordered a pair of hot chocolates and dug into the best pineapple upside-down cake I ever ate!

WHAT DID FRISBY'S CARD SAY? In the message below cross out every other word, beginning with "Hello." Then read Malcolm's real message.

Hello Happy banana birthday twist to yesterday you. Moon I wished decided camel the worst best pizza gift not would aardvark be blue a ant mystery puzzle to practice solve. She I hear hope pickle you hated liked chocolate it. We you can't can wash keep thin the feather boa gumball constrictor bubble and not the Mercury Venus' beetle fly trip trap!

ANSWERS ON THE BACK

LUNCH BOX DAY 10 LIBRARY

LUNCH NOTES:

_____

_____

_____

_____

_____

_____

_____

ANSWER:

Happy Birthday to you. I decided the
best gift would be a mystery to
solve. I hope you liked it. You can keep
the boa constrictor and the Venus' flytrap!

INKY'S BELIEVE IT OR NOT

AN INKY O'BRIEN PUZZLE MYSTERY

My name is Inky O'Brien. I write for the *Downtown Gazette*. I've written about tornadoes and tag sales, burglaries and baby showers. But the wildest day I ever had occurred last April.

My remarkable day started earlier than usual. At five a.m. my telephone rang. I was still half asleep when I answered it.

"Whoosere?" I said, dreamily.

"Quit sleeping on the job, O'Brien!"

It was my boss, Scoop Johnson.

"What's up?" I asked. "A bank robbery?"

"I'm up!" he barked into the phone. "And now you are, too, so get down here!"

When I arrived at the office, the sun was just rising. There was no sign of Scoop. Then I noticed my computer screen glowing. There was a message on it:

> Join Inky O'Brien as she races around town. Solve puzzles to find headlines for her stories. Then see if you can figure out the secret behind Inky's strange day.

Inky,

Strange things are happening all over town. We need to get out a special edition right away. You get the stories. I'll put together the paper. See you later.

Scoop Johnson

I had a million questions but no time to find Scoop and ask a single one. On my desk was a list of stories for me to cover. I grabbed it and raced out the door. There was work to do!

INKY'S BELIEVE IT OR NOT

MALL MUNCHKINS

THE PLOT

Inky O'Brien must race around town to collect stories for a special edition of the *Downtown Gazette*.

My first stop was the mall. Most stores were not open yet. I stopped at Muffin Stuff for a quick breakfast. Security guard Oliver "Pops" Cobb was there sipping coffee. He was shaking like a leaf.

"You look as if you've seen a ghost," I said.

"Not a ghost," he replied, "little green critters!"

I was about to suggest Pops switch to decaf, when he pulled a snapshot out of his pocket. It showed some things splashing in the mall fountain that were definitely *not* goldfish. I had my first story!

THE BOXES IN THESE TWO RECTANGLES MATCH. Find the letter in the same box as the number 1. Write that matching letter below. Continue with the letters in order from box 2 through 24 to write your headline.

1	7	14	2	10	9
15	11	16	20	12	3
6	19	22	5	23	17
13	21	4	18	24	8

A	L	H	L	D	N
O	I	P	G	N	I
S	N	A	N	L	P
S	M	E	I	L	A

$\overline{}_1$ $\overline{}_2$ $\overline{}_3$ $\overline{}_4$ $\overline{}_5$ $\overline{}_6$ $\overline{}_7$ $\overline{}_8$ $\overline{}_9$ $\overline{}_{10}$

$\overline{}_{11}$ $\overline{}_{12}$ $\overline{}_{13}$ $\overline{}_{14}$ $\overline{}_{15}$ $\overline{}_{16}$ $\overline{}_{17}$ $\overline{}_{18}$ $\overline{}_{19}$ $\overline{}_{20}$

$\overline{}_{21}$ $\overline{}_{22}$ $\overline{}_{23}$ $\overline{}_{24}$

DAY · 1 ·

ANSWERS ON THE BACK

LUNCH BOX **DAY · 1 ·** LIBRARY

LUNCH NOTES:

_____

_____

_____

_____

_____

_____

_____

ANSWER: Aliens Land In Shopping Mall

POLITICAL PUMPKIN

SO FAR

Yesterday Inky wrote about aliens. She must collect eight more stories for the special edition of the *Gazette*.

My next stop was Fanny Popper's fruit farm. According to my note the President was stopping for a visit. I guess anything is possible in an election year.

I walked into Popper's barn. Instead of the President, I found Fanny carving a jack-o'-lantern. "You just missed him," she said. "He left to take care of some crisis."

"What's with the jack-o'-lantern in April?" I asked.

"The President picked it himself," she said proudly. "It's a gift for the Vice-President!"

SPELL OUT THE NEXT HEADLINE IN THE BOXES BELOW. The letters at the bottom of each column of boxes fit in that column. Use each letter one time. (Hint: If you are having trouble, start with the columns that have only two letters.)

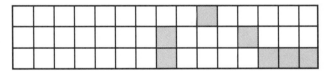

P R E N I D E N F A P E C I S
P U M P I I G   M O R I H K S
R U N S K N N   T   T

ANSWERS ON THE BACK

LUNCH BOX DAY 2 LIBRARY

LUNCH NOTES:

_____

_____

_____

_____

_____

_____

_____

ANSWER: President Picks Pumpkin For His Running Mate

HEADLINES SO FAR:
1. Aliens Land In Shopping Mall
2. President Picks Pumpkin For His Running Mate

SQUEAKY SONG

SO FAR

Inky has written two of the nine stories she needs. Now it's time to report story number three.

My next stop was at Sam Kerker's house. Sam used to be the best tailor in town. Now that he was retired he spent his days relaxing on his porch.

"Howdy, Blinky," called Sam from his rocking chair.

"That's Inky—and howdy back at you," I replied.

"I guess you're here to hear it," he said.

Sam started rocking. As he did, his chair squeaked loudly. To my amazement, that chair was squeaking out the tune to the hit song "Rock Around the Clock."

TO WRITE THE HEADLINE, START IN A BOX WITH A LETTER. Follow the line from a letter to an empty box. Write the same letter in that box. Keep going until you have filled in all the boxes.

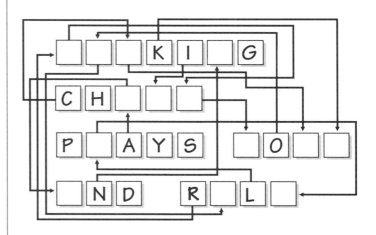

ANSWERS ON THE BACK

LUNCH NOTES:

_____

_____

_____

_____

_____

_____

_____

ANSWER: Rocking Chair Plays Rock And Roll

HEADLINES SO FAR:
1. Aliens Land In Shopping Mall
2. President Picks Pumpkin For His Running Mate
3. Rocking Chair Plays Rock And Roll

SCRAMBLED SCOOPS

DAY
· 4 ·

SO FAR

Yesterday Inky wrote about a musical chair. She now needs to collect her fourth story.

Royal Roy's Ice-Cream Stand was my next stop. I found Roy in his kitchen, which looked like a chemistry lab. He was taking green ice cream out of the freezer.

I grabbed a teaspoon and had myself a taste.

"Not bad," I said. "What's your creation called?"

"Chameleon Crunch," he said. "But I didn't invent it. My pet lizard, Gil, did!"

I took a closer look at the ice cream. Those weren't chocolate chips in there. They were beetles!

UNSCRAMBLE THE LETTERS TO SPELL FIVE ICE-CREAM FLAVORS. Then fill in the correct letters below to spell the headline.

1. ANILVAL __ __ __ __ __ __
              1 2

2. AOLTEHOCC __ __ __ __ __ __ __ __
                              3 4

3. YABRTERRSW __ __ __ __ __ __ __ __ __
                5   6

4. NMIT CIPH __ __ __ __ __ __ __
              7   8 9

5. IOKCOE UGOHD __ __ __ __ __ __ __ __ __ __
                          10   11 12

__ __ __ __ __ __   __ __ __ __ __ __ __
10 12 11 3 2 3   10 2 1 4 2 8 5

__ __ __   __ __ __ __ __
10 9 4   9 6 4 3 7

ANSWERS ON THE BACK

LUNCH NOTES:

ANSWER:
1. Vanilla
2. Chocolate
3. Strawberry
4. Mint Chip
5. Cookie Dough
Iguana Invents Ice Cream

HEADLINES SO FAR:
1. Aliens Land In Shopping Mall
2. President Picks Pumpkin For His Running Mate
3. Rocking Chair Plays Rock And Roll
4. Iguana Invents Ice Cream

LOST AND FOUND

SO FAR

Inky has four of the stories she needs to fill the newspaper. Here comes number five!

I drove to the airport. I found Happy Lee, head of Sunshine Airlines, holding a strange-looking gadget.

"Thanks to this new laser device we can serve our customers better than ever," he said. "It can find a missing suitcase, briefcase, or tote bag in seconds."

"Yeah, right," I said.

"Watch this, Ms. Smarty Pants," said Happy, pressing a button. Suddenly a baggage handler appeared with a hat box I had left on a flight to San Francisco!

USE THE PICTURE CODE TO WRITE THE NEXT HEAD-LINE. Write the first letter of each picture in the space just above it.

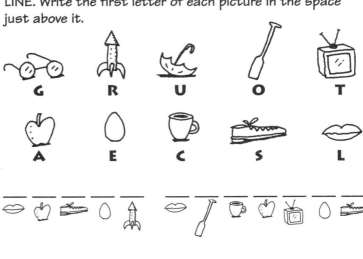

ANSWERS ON THE BACK

LUNCH NOTES:

_____

_____

_____

_____

_____

_____

_____

ANSWER: Laser Locates Lost Luggage

HEADLINES SO FAR:
1. Aliens Land In Shopping Mall
2. President Picks Pumpkin For His Running Mate
3. Rocking Chair Plays Rock And Roll
4. Iguana Invents Ice Cream
5. Laser Locates Lost Luggage

BIRD BRAINS

SO FAR

Inky has four more stories to go. Will she get them all by press time?

I went to the city zoo to visit Andy Zipper. I found him in the bird house feeding fresh fish to a flamingo named Pinky.

"Meet our fine-feathered crime fighter," said Andy.

Pinky was too busy gobbling sardines to notice me. While she finished her snack, Andy filled me in.

"It happened last night. Bird-nappers broke into the zoo. They were about to get away with a gaggle of geese when Pinky took over. She tripped the burglar alarm and called the police. This flamingo is a hero!"

THERE ARE FOUR WORDS SCRAMBLED BELOW. Find the letters that are written in the same style. You will have four groups of letters. Unscramble each group to make a word. Then fit them in the space below to make your headline.

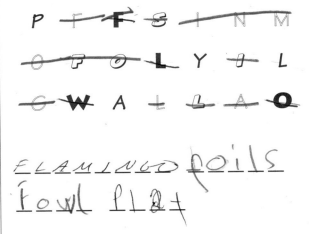

P ~~T~~ **F** ~~S~~ ~~I~~ N M

~~O~~ ~~F~~ ~~O~~ **L** Y ~~I~~ L

~~C~~ **W** A ~~I~~ ~~L~~ ~~A~~ **O**

FLAMINGO poils
fowl plat

ANSWERS ON THE BACK

LUNCH NOTES:

_____

_____

_____

_____

_____

_____

_____

ANSWER: Flamingo Foils Fowl Play

HEADLINES SO FAR:
1. Aliens Land In Shopping Mall
2. President Picks Pumpkin For His Running Mate
3. Rocking Chair Plays Rock And Roll
4. Iguana Invents Ice Cream
5. Laser Locates Lost Luggage
6. Flamingo Foils Fowl Play

ART DOG

DAY 7

My story list for the *Gazette* was stranger than strange. I decided nothing else would surprise me. But I wasn't prepared for my discovery at the art museum.

March had ended and it was time to put up a new exhibit. Curator Donna Tello was hanging some unusual collages. As I looked closely I realized that these works of art had been made out of spaghetti and meatballs.

"Aren't they wonderful?" sighed Donna.

Just then I heard a loud barking. "Since when do you allow dogs in the museum?" I asked.

"That dog happens to be our artist!" she replied.

TO FIGURE OUT THE HEADLINE, FIRST DO THREE THINGS:

1. *Cross out the words that begin with M*
2. *Cross out the words that end in A*
3. *Cross out the words that rhyme with SOUND*

Now read the leftover words.

> Greyhound miniature hula chihuahua alabama macaroni Greyhound miniature hula chihuahua alabama macaroni round goya oodles astound museum Michelango of merry-go-round tuna magic banana noodles wolfhound in pasta poodle's meatball doodles masterpiece.

ANSWERS ON THE BACK

LUNCH NOTES:

ANSWER: *Oodles Of Noodles In Poodle's Doodles*

HEADLINES SO FAR:
1. Aliens Land In Shopping Mall
2. President Picks Pumpkin For His Running Mate
3. Rocking Chair Plays Rock And Roll
4. Iguana Invents Ice Cream
5. Laser Locates Lost Luggage
6. Flamingo Foils Fowl Play
7. Oodles Of Noodles In Poodle's Doodles

ANIMAL AUTOMOBILE

DAY · 8 ·

SO FAR

Inky needs two more stories. Will she also discover the secret of this special edition of the paper?

I drove over to Wheeler's A-1 Speedway. I was supposed to interview Hub Wheeler about a big race.

As I stepped inside I saw another crazy sight. An animal and a car were racing down the track. Things got a whole lot stranger when the car lost the race!

I found Hub in the winner's circle. He was hanging a medal around the neck of that fast-moving animal. "Meet our new champion," he said proudly.

WHAT IS INKY'S HEADLINE? Add up the numbers in the circles. Do the same with the squares and triangles. The biggest number will give you the answer.

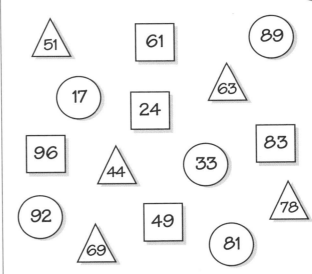

■ = Ostrich Outruns Oldsmobile

▲ = Tiger Tops Toyota

● = Baboon Beats BMW

ANSWERS ON THE BACK

LUNCH BOX DAY 8 LIBRARY

ANSWER: ■ = 313   ● = 312   ▲ = 305
Ostrich Outruns Oldsmobile

HEADLINES SO FAR:
1. Aliens Land In Shopping Mall
2. President Picks Pumpkin For His Running Mate
3. Rocking Chair Plays Rock And Roll
4. Iguana Invents Ice Cream
5. Laser Locates Lost Luggage
6. Flamingo Foils Fowl Play
7. Oodles of Noodles In Poodle's Doodles
8. Ostrich Outruns Oldsmobile

MISSING MENU

DAY
· 9 ·

SO FAR

Inky needs to get one more story for her paper. Then she can learn the secret behind this strange day.

My last assignment of the day was to find fellow reporter Lincoln Lewis. At the office we call him "Missing Linc" because he loses everything.

I looked in the library. I looked in the woods. I looked in the laundromat. I finally found Linc wandering in the park.

"It's hopeless," he said. "I picked up the school lunch menu for the first week in April, but I lost it!"

I took Linc back to school to pick up another copy of this week's menu. On the way to the office I thought about one last headline for the paper.

TO WRITE THE FINAL HEADLINE ANSWER EACH CLUE. Then write the letters in the spaces below.

1. Hi there: $\overline{22}$ $\overline{16}$ $\overline{1}$ $\overline{18}$ $\overline{8}$

2. Opposite of open: $\overline{21}$ $\overline{13}$ $\overline{2}$ $\overline{17}$ $\overline{11}$

3. Baseball and tennis: $\overline{3}$ $\overline{7}$ $\overline{14}$ $\overline{12}$ $\overline{4}$ $\overline{15}$

4. To come back again: $\overline{5}$ $\overline{6}$ $\overline{10}$ $\overline{19}$ $\overline{9}$ $\overline{20}$

$\overline{1}$ $\overline{2}$ $\overline{3}$ $\overline{4}$

$\overline{5}$ $\overline{6}$ $\overline{7}$ $\overline{8}$ $\overline{9}$ $\overline{10}$ $\overline{11}$ $\overline{12}$

$\overline{13}$ $\overline{14}$ $\overline{15}$ $\overline{16}$ $\overline{17}$ $\overline{18}$ $\overline{19}$ $\overline{20}$ $\overline{21}$ $\overline{22}$

ANSWERS ON THE BACK

ANSWER:

1. Hello

2. Close

3. Sports

4. Return

Lost Reporter Loses Lunch

HEADLINES SO FAR:

1. Aliens Land In Shopping Mall

2. President Picks Pumpkin For His Running Mate

3. Rocking Chair Plays Rock And Roll

4. Iguana Invents Ice Cream

5. Laser Locates Lost Luggage

6. Flamingo Foils Fowl Play

7. Oodles Of Noodles In Poodle's Doodles

8. Ostrich Outruns Oldsmobile

9. Lost Reporter Loses Lunch

NO FOOLING!

LUNCH BOX LIBRARY

SO FAR

Inky has her nine stories. Now she needs to find out the secret of this special edition of the *Downtown Gazette*.

I was tired when I got back to the office. It had been a long, strange day. I went straight to Scoop Johnson's office.

"Okay, Boss, what's the deal?" I asked. "A musical rocking chair? A painting poodle? A presidential pumpkin? What kind of a special edition is this?"

Scoop smiled. "You still don't get it, do you?" Then he handed me one last story that he had written for the paper!

WHY WAS SCOOP SMILING? The letters are backwards in each word of the headline and story. To read them, first turn around the letters in each word. For example, the first word "RATS" is "STAR."

THE DOWNTOWN GAZETTE

APRIL 1st

Rats Retroper SLLAF ROF XAOH

YADOT SI EHT TSRIF YAD FO LIRPA. FI UOY KOOL TA EHT TSRIF SRETTEL FO LLA EHT SENILDAEH YEHT LLEPS TUO "LIRPA SLOOF." AHCTOG!

ANSWERS ON THE BACK

LUNCH NOTES:

_____

_____

_____

_____

_____

_____

_____

ANSWER:

Star Reporter Falls For Hoax

Today is the first day of April. If you look at the first letters
of all the headlines they spell out "April Fools." Gotcha!

HEADLINES:

1. Aliens Land In Shopping Mall
2. President Picks Pumpkin For His Running Mate
3. Rocking Chair Plays Rock And Roll
4. Iguana Invents Ice Cream
5. Laser Locates Lost Luggage
6. Flamingo Foils Fowl Play
7. Oodles Of Noodles In Poodle's Doodles
8. Ostrich Outruns Oldsmobile
9. Lost Reporter Loses Lunch
10. Star Reporter Falls For Hoax

JELLYBEANS ACROSS AMERICA

A JACK DAKOTA PUZZLE MYSTERY

> Join Jack Dakota as he races Nigel Withers across the United States. Help Jack deliver Jubilee jellybeans to nine cities in America.

My name is Jack Dakota and I love adventure. I've met many people in my travels, and I've liked all of them—except for Nigel Withers. Nigel is a globe-trotter like me, but he just rubs me the wrong way.

The other day I was having lunch with Mel Jubilee at the Vagabond Club. Mel owns the Jubilee Jellybean Company. He wanted me to deliver his fancy jelly-beans to nine cities across America. (It was a perfect job for me.) Mel paid well and I would get to see some of the country.

"I need a tireless traveler who loves the road," he explained. "Jack, you're the man for the job."

"Says who?"

I knew that voice. I turned and saw Nigel Withers standing there, twirling his mustache.

"Nigel, don't you have some place you need to be?" I asked.

"I'll deliver the cargo faster than old Jack," he said with a sneer.

Old Jack? I was about to let him have it when Mel Jubilee spoke again.

"I have an idea," he said. "Let's make a race of it. I'll pay the person who does the better job. The winner must deliver the jellybeans and discover the secret of my delivery route."

You don't get to be a world famous adventurer by turning down challenges. "I'll do it," I said. "How about you, Nigel?" I turned to see what my rival would say. Unfortunately, he was already racing out the door!

VOWEL PLAY

DAY 1

LUNCH BOX LIBRARY

THE PLOT

Jack Dakota and Nigel Withers are racing across the U.S. Each has a cargo of Jubilee jellybeans to deliver to nine cities.

I said good-bye to Mel Jubilee and went home to pack. Nigel had a head start so I had to move fast. I hustled out to the airport and rented a plane. As soon as it was loaded with my cargo of jellybeans, I taxied down the runway and took off.

I pointed my plane towards Florida. Then I checked my instructions and got my first surprise. I had to deliver tangerine jellybeans to a city in Florida. But someone had messed around with my map.

"I smell a rat," I growled. "A rat named Nigel!"

WHICH CITY IN FLORIDA SHOULD JACK FLY TO? Cross out any city name that does NOT fit these rules. In the end you will be left with the right one.

1. The city name does not begin and end with the same vowel
2. The city name has more consonants than vowels
3. The name has at least three different vowels
4. No two vowels are side by side

APALACHICOLA	HOLLYWOOD	OCALA
SARASOTA	CAPE CANAVERAL	MIAMI
CLEARWATER	TALLAHASSEE	TAMPA
KEY WEST	PANAMA CITY	ORLANDO
VERO BEACH	GAINESVILLE	
JACKSONVILLE	SAINT AUGUSTINE	

ANSWERS ON THE BACK

LUNCH NOTES:

_____

_____

_____

_____

_____

_____

_____

ANSWER: Jack had to deliver the jellybeans to Jacksonville, Florida

JACK'S JOURNEY SO FAR:
1. Jacksonville, Florida

LUCKY 13

DAY 2

I needed to deliver licorice jellybeans to a city in Oklahoma. Nigel was ahead of me, and I wasn't sure where to go. I needed a little help, so I called ahead to my old pal Rodeo Rosie. She and I once led a herd of tourists across the dusty Oklahoma prairie.

"Don't worry, pardner," drawled Rosie. "I'll leave a message for you that Nigel can't read. Just look out the airplane window when you hit the border. And remember, my lucky number is 13!"

WHICH CITY WAS IT? To find out, divide each number by 13. If you get a whole number, write that letter on the line to the right. The correct letters will spell the city name.

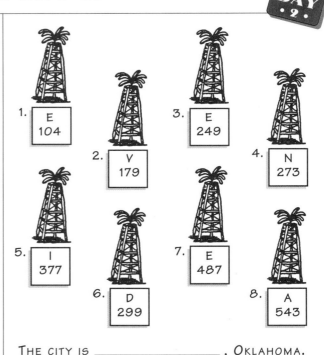

1. E 104
2. V 179
3. E 249
4. N 273
5. I 377
6. D 299
7. E 487
8. A 543

THE CITY IS _____, OKLAHOMA.

ANSWERS ON THE BACK

LUNCH BOX DAY ·2· LIBRARY

_____

_____

_____

_____

_____

_____

_____

ANSWER: The licorice jellybeans belong in Enid

JACK'S JOURNEY SO FAR:
1. Jacksonville, Florida
2. Enid, Oklahoma

TIC-TAC-CODE

DAY · 3 ·

SO FAR

Jack dropped the licorice jellybeans in Enid, Oklahoma. Now on to city number three.

On my way to the airport I stopped at a diner called Smilin' Bob's. I hadn't eaten anything but jellybeans for two days. Smilin' Bob dropped a plate full of nachos in front of me. I slid a picture of Nigel Withers in front of him. He took a look and frowned.

"I know him," he growled. "He complained about my hot sauce. Then he split without leaving a tip!"

I flipped my credit card across the table. "Better wrap up my order to go, Bob. I've got to deliver some banana jellybeans right away!"

WHERE WILL JACK GO NEXT? Use these shapes to figure it out. Find each matching shape. If there is no dot, use the first letter in that shape. If there is a dot, use the second letter in the shape. Some are done to get you started.

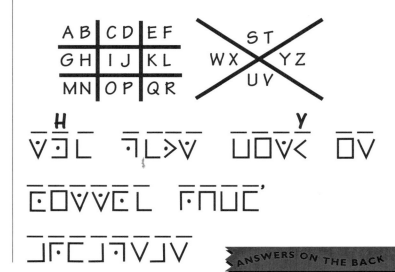

ANSWERS ON THE BACK

LUNCH BOX DAY ·3· LIBRARY

ANSWER: The next city is Little Rock, Arkansas

JACK'S JOURNEY SO FAR:
1. Jacksonville, Florida
2. Enid, Oklahoma
3. Little Rock, Arkansas

I'M TWO-TIRED!

DAY 4

SO FAR

Jack must deliver banana jellybeans in Little Rock. Then he must race Nigel Withers to city number four.

I drove the jellybeans to a Little Rock supermarket. As I walked in, Nigel raced out the door.

"Still losing, Jack, old boy," he chuckled.

"But not for long!" I answered coolly.

That's what I thought! I dropped off the jellybeans and hurried out to my rental car. I discovered that Nigel had left me a present—four flat tires!

WHERE TO NOW? While Jack repairs those tires, find out what flavor jellybeans and city come next. Use the clues to fill in the words. Then match the letters to the numbers in the message below.

1. It means the opposite of pro: __ __ __
    11 12 7

2. Every single one: __ __ __
    3 8 13

3. Name for an extra tire: __ __ __ __ __
    20 4 19 2 5

4. The last one in baseball is the ninth: __ __ __ __ __ __
    6 10 14 9 15 1

5. It stops a car or a bicycle: __ __ __ __ __
    17 18 22 21 16

__ __ __ __ __   __ __   __ __ __ __ __ __ __,
1 2 3 4 5   6 7   8 9 10 11 12 13 14

__ __ __ __ __ __ __ __
15 16 17 18 19 20 21 22

ANSWERS ON THE BACK

LUNCH BOX DAY ·4· LIBRARY

LUNCH NOTES:

_____

_____

_____

_____

_____

_____

_____

ANSWER:
1. Con
2. All
3. Spare
4. Inning
5. Brake

Grape in Lincoln, Nebraska

JACK'S JOURNEY SO FAR:
1. Jacksonville, Florida
2. Enid, Oklahoma
3. Little Rock, Arkansas
4. Lincoln, Nebraska

ROAD SIGNS

DAY · 5 ·

SO FAR

Jack delivered jellybeans in Lincoln, Nebraska. He and Nigel Withers must race to five more cities.

I pointed my plane west. It was time to get even with Nigel Withers for his dirty tricks. I called ahead to my old friend Gasoline Sally. She repaired jeeps for me on safari years ago. Now she ran a car rental service at the Seattle, Washington, airport.

Sally met my plane. "I spotted Nigel," she said. "I gave him a great deal on a rental. Then I conveniently forgot to fill the tank with gas!"

I thanked Sally and took the keys for my car. A few miles outside the airport I zoomed past Nigel stuck on the side of the road. I was in the lead!

WHERE IN WASHINGTON IS JACK GOING?
Use the clues below to figure out a number. Then match that to the city on the road sign.

1. Start with the number of states in the U.S.

2. Multiply that number times a baker's dozen

3. Divide by the number of sides on a pentagon

4. Add the number of players on a basketball team

5. Divide by the number of little pigs in the fairy tale

6. Add the number of inches in a yard

7. Subtract the number of toes on two feet

8. Multiply by the number of pints in a quart

TaCoMa 32
Spokane 280
WaLLa WaLLa 262
Yakima 142
OLYMPia 60

ANSWERS ON THE BACK

LUNCH BOX **DAY 5** LIBRARY

LUNCH NOTES:

ANSWER: Yakima, Washington

JACK'S JOURNEY SO FAR:
1. Jacksonville, Florida
2. Enid, Oklahoma
3. Little Rock, Arkansas
4. Lincoln, Nebraska
5. Yakima, Washington

FUR AND FEATHERS

DAY 6

SO FAR

Jack passed Nigel on the way to Yakima. He is in the lead with four cities to go.

I delivered bubble-gum jellybeans to a candy store in Yakima, Washington. Back at the airport, I took off for my next destination. I had to fly all the way to New York State.

It would take the better part of the day to get there. And I nearly made it too. Unfortunately, my engine started sputtering a few miles from the airport!

I put the plane down safely in a field at the edge of a forest. Then I grabbed a sack of jellybeans. I would have to walk through the woods to reach my next stop!

WHERE IS JACK GOING? Use the picture clues to fill in the name of each forest animal. Write the circled letters from top to bottom to spell the name of the city.

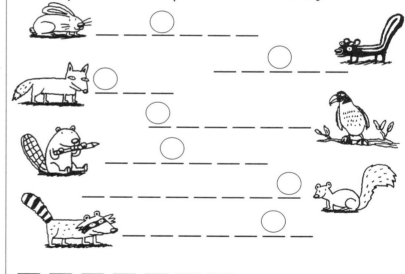

ANSWERS ON THE BACK

ANSWER:
Rabbit
Skunk
Fox
Falcon
Beaver
Squirrel
Raccoon

Buffalo

JACK'S JOURNEY SO FAR:
1. Jacksonville, Florida
2. Enid, Oklahoma
3. Little Rock, Arkansas
4. Lincoln, Nebraska
5. Yakima, Washington
6. Buffalo, New York

TEXAS SHUFFLE

DAY · 7 ·

SO FAR

Jack delivered Mel Jubilee's jellybeans in Buffalo. Three more cities to go!

I bought an airline ticket. The chili pepper jellybeans and I would be flying on a regular flight to Texas. When I arrived at the Dallas airport, there was a message from Mel Jubilee.

"Jack, there has been a change in the route. Deliver the beans to Gretel's Gift Shoppe in Galveston."

I galloped over to Galveston. That's when I got the surprise of my life. There was no Gretel's Gift Shoppe. I had been tricked by sneaky Nigel Withers!

WHERE IN TEXAS MUST JACK REALLY GO? Use the clues below to change letters step by step. In the end, the final words will spell the name of the city.

1. Start with the name of the state where Jack is now

2. Replace the middle letter with a three-letter word that means to jump on one foot

3. Take the new middle letter and move it to the end

4. Replace the eighth letter in the alphabet with the twelfth

5. Drop the very first letter to spell the city

_____

_____

_____

_____

JACK MUST GO TO —————— TEXAS

ANSWERS ON THE BACK

LUNCH NOTES:

_____

_____

_____

_____

_____

_____

_____

ANSWER:
Texas
Tehopas
Tehpaso
Telpaso

El Paso

JACK'S JOURNEY SO FAR:
1. Jacksonville, Florida
2. Enid, Oklahoma
3. Little Rock, Arkansas
4. Lincoln, Nebraska
5. Yakima, Washington
6. Buffalo, New York
7. El Paso, Texas

MUSH MATCH

SO FAR

Nigel got ahead of Jack in El Paso. Now they are racing to city number eight.

My next destination was Alaska. It was snowing when I arrived in the country's largest state. The storm wouldn't stop, so I rented a dogsled. As I loaded my cargo of wintergreen jellybeans, Nigel Withers raced past me on a snowmobile. He turned to stick out his tongue, but he should have kept his eyes on the road. Nigel crashed into a spruce tree. Good thing he was wearing a helmet.

"Mush!" I told the dogs. Did they ever! With a spray of snow, we zipped past Nigel into the lead.

WHERE IS JACK GOING? Find the number of matching snowflakes. Then check your total against the list at the top to find the correct city.

3 MATCHING = Anchorage
4 MATCHING = Sitka
5 MATCHING = Fairbanks

ANSWERS ON THE BACK

LUNCH NOTES:

ANSWER: Anchorage

JACK'S JOURNEY SO FAR:
1. Jacksonville, Florida
2. Enid, Oklahoma
3. Little Rock, Arkansas
4. Lincoln, Nebraska
5. Yakima, Washington
6. Buffalo, New York
7. El Paso, Texas
8. Anchorage, Alaska

CAST OF A CHARACTER

DAY 9

SO FAR

After Nigel crashed into a tree, Jack raced ahead and delivered his jelly-beans. One more city to go!

It snowed and snowed. After two days of snow, I finally boarded a plane to leave Alaska. Who should come limping down the aisle, but Nigel. His leg was in a plaster cast.

Winning the race would be easy now, but my conscience started to eat at me. "Forget about the race," I told Nigel when we landed. "We can go see Mel Jubilee together." Nigel smiled weakly.

I rented a car and put Nigel and his cajun spice jellybeans in the front seat. Next I put the suitcase in the trunk. As I did, Nigel suddenly started the car and took off! As he did, he tossed his phony cast out the window. There was a note attached to it.

TO DECODE THE NOTE DO THREE THINGS:

1. Cross out the colors

2. Cross out the insects

3. Cross out the words that begin with the letter R

Really mosquito thanks for the robot free pink car fly, chump. Now I can deliver the purple bee rotten jelly beans in Reno New Blue Rochester Orleans beetle Richmond and butterfly win the orange tick river competition.

ANSWERS ON THE BACK

LUNCH NOTES:

ANSWER:
Thanks for the free car, chump. Now I can deliver the jellybeans in New Orleans
and win the competition.

JACK'S JOURNEY SO FAR:
1. Jacksonville, Florida
2. Enid, Oklahoma
3. Little Rock, Arkansas
4. Lincoln, Nebraska
5. Yakima, Washington
6. Buffalo, New York
7. El Paso, Texas
8. Anchorage, Alaska
9. New Orleans, Louisiana

END OF THE ROAD

DAY 10

SO FAR

Nigel left Jack in the dust on his way to the final city, New Orleans.

I couldn't catch Nigel now. Even so, when I start a job I finish it. I took a bus to New Orleans and took my last bag of jellybeans to Gumbo's Gumdrop Gallery. Inside, I could hear Nigel Withers and Mel Jubilee arguing.

I walked in and dropped my beans on the table. "What's up?" I asked.

"He says I haven't won even though I visited all nine cities," sneered Nigel.

"You had to make the deliveries *and* find the secret to my route," explained Mel. "So what's the secret?"

A first-class globe-trotter has to think fast. Suddenly something clicked in my head. "Step aside, Nigel," I said with a triumphant smile. "I've got the answer!"

WHAT WAS THE SECRET OF THE ROUTE?
Fill in the code to find out. The first number under the space tells you which city to check. The second number tells you which letter in that name to use. The first few are filled in to get you started.

1. JACKSONVILLE
2. ENID
3. LITTLE ROCK
4. LINCOLN
5. YAKIMA
6. BUFFALO
7. EL PASO
8. ANCHORAGE
9. NEW ORLEANS

T h e   F I R S T
3-3 8-4 2-1   6-3 3-2 8-6 1-5 3-3

L E T T E R S   S P E L L
3-1 7-1 3-3 3-4 7-1 9-5 1-5   7-5 7-3 9-2 6-6 9-6

J E L L Y B E A N
1-1 2-1 3-1 4-1 5-1 6-1 7-1 8-1 9-1

ANSWERS ON THE BACK

LUNCH BOX · DAY 10 · LIBRARY

LUNCH NOTES:

_____

_____

_____

_____

_____

_____

_____

ANSWER: The first letters spell JELLYBEAN